Mrs. J. H. Riddell

Susan Drummond

A Novel. Vol. 2

Mrs. J. H. Riddell

Susan Drummond
A Novel. Vol. 2

ISBN/EAN: 9783337046347

Printed in Europe, USA, Canada, Australia, Japan

Cover: Foto ©Andreas Hilbeck / pixelio.de

More available books at **www.hansebooks.com**

SUSAN DRUMMOND.

A Novel.

BY

MRS. J. H. RIDDELL,

AUTHOR OF "THE SENIOR PARTNER," "GEORGE GEITH, OF FEN COURT," ETC.

IN THREE VOLUMES.

VOL. II.

LONDON:

RICHARD BENTLEY & SON, NEW BURLINGTON STREET.

Publishers in Ordinary to Her Majesty the Queen.

1884.

CONTENTS.

SUSAN DRUMMOND.

CHAPTER I.

SIR GEOFFREY'S OPINIONS.

PPARENTLY Mr. Gayre found his subject less easy than it seemed at first mention, for, instead of proceeding to say what he had to say, he repeated his former statement in a different form.

"Believe me, I played eavesdropper quite unintentionally. It was impossible for me to help hearing your conversation."

"No," answered Susan, varying her monosyllable, but not its sense. "It does not matter in the least," she went on, imagining Mr. Gayre intended to convey some sort of apology. "Lal spoke loud enough for all the world to hear."

The banker laughed. "That is quite true," he said. "Of course, Miss Drummond, it would be both impertinent and intrusive were I to make any remark on Mr. Hilderton's words. All I want to say is—"

"Don't say anything hard about poor Lal," she interrupted. "He is trying at times ; but so few people understand him."

"I think I do."

"No, indeed, you cannot. Even to-night, for instance—" and then Lal's champion paused suddenly.

"Even to-night, for instance?" repeated Mr. Gayre, with quiet suggestiveness.

"I dislike half sentences, and yet I cannot finish mine," said Susan. "I may tell you this much, however," she added, "that the day's festivities have tried his not particularly equable temper a good deal.

After all, if you think over the position, it cannot be pleasant for a poor man who does possess genius to mix amongst people incapable of recognising genius till it is successful!"

"You bring me to the very point I wanted to reach," replied the banker. "I wish to help Mr. Hilderton to make the genius he undoubtedly possesses profitable; but I scarcely know how to set about the matter. He is a little 'difficult.'"

"Not a little—very," amended Susan. "So difficult, that I really sometimes fail to see how even his best friends are to put him in the straight road for fortune."

"I am quite willing to try, if you assist me with a few hints. Knowing the interest—the *great* interest—you take in Mr. Hilderton's future, it would give me the sincerest pleasure to aid him by any means in my power."

"I certainly like Lal," answered Susan

slowly, struck by something in her companion's tone—something implied which she instinctively felt she ought to show him she understood—" very much indeed ; both for his own sake, and on account of old times ; but—"

" I suppose one cannot expect a young lady to say more," Mr. Gayre observed, almost as if by way of inquiry.

" I hope, Mr. Gayre, you do not imagine for a moment—"

" What, Miss Drummond ?"

" That I care for Mr. Hilderton excepting as a friend? A dear friend, of course ; but one who could never by any possibility be more to me." Susan was a little angry, and spoke with a plain decision no man could really have misinterpreted.

Mr. Gayre did not, at all events, though it suited his purpose to ask.

" And why should I not imagine he might some day be more to you ?"

"Because," she answered, "I thought you knew me better."

Just for a moment there came a wild temptation over him to say he did, to cast his arms around her and strain her to his heart, and then and there, under the silent stars, with lights gleaming through the open windows above, and music floating down to where they stood, tell the tale of how love in middle age had come to him, and made life all beautiful and good and sweet, since a certain May day, when for the first time he saw, in Hyde Park, Susan Drummond's fair dear face calmly watching the antics of Squire Temperley's hunter.

But he was prudent; he did know her so well that he felt sure, if the faintest consciousness of liking him over-much had entered her mind, those charming lips would never have spoken the words which filled his heart with such delight. He would wait; he would not frighten, even by a gesture, this innocent, fearless, winsome bird, which seemed inclined to flutter towards him and settle on his hand.

"To be quite candid," he answered, and in his voice there was no trace of the strong constraint he put on his speech, " I thought I *did* know you better. It was an idea which would never have entered my own mind; but Mrs. Jubbins felt so sure, so satisfied—"

" Dear, kind Mrs. Jubbins," murmured Susan. " She has indeed been good to Lal."

" Then there is really nothing in the affair ? "

" Nothing whatever ; nothing on either side," she said eagerly, yet with pretty confusion. " Still, none the less, Mr. Gayre, you will help him, won't you ? "

None the less ! If she could only have read his soul she would have understood all the more—a thousand times the more.

"I will do my best, my very best for him," answered the banker earnestly; "but you must help me, Miss Drummond. You will teach me how to give him hints and avoid offence."

"Not a very easy task," she declared; "but I will try to teach you the geography of that very strange country, Lionel Hilderton's mind; that is to say, so far as I may," she added, with an unintentional significance. "And now you must not say I am like a child who does not know what it wants if I ask you to take me in again. I feel as much too cold as I did too warm ten minutes ago. The night air out here is chilly."

"Wrap your shawl closer around you," said Mr. Gayre anxiously. "I am afraid you are not well. You have been over-exciting yourself."

"Perhaps I have a little," she agreed; "but that is nothing, and I feel so much happier, so very much happier, since we talked about Lal. I do not know how to thank you enough ; I do not indeed."

Mr. Gayre could have told her ; but once again he refrained. Who would willingly, even for reality, break the soft spell of such a dream as the man then revelled in ?

"And so," to change the subject, he said, looking up at The Warren, " you think Love would not be a suitable tenant for Lady Merioneth's cottage ? "

"Well, you see," explained Susan, leaning a little on his arm as they ascended the slope, her head bent somewhat back, her eyes scanning the long terrace and the brilliantly-lighted windows, " the poets, so far as I can remember, have never yet represented Love as a Millionaire."

"What do you think of Mr. Sudlow as combining both characters?"

"I may be wrong," she answered, " but

I fancy he feels his position as a rich man too much to act the part of Cupid very naturally."

" And yet he is deeply smitten with my niece."

" So I see," Susan agreed ; and they proceeded a dozen steps or more in silence.

They were slowly ascending towards the house. Mingling with the tones of the music they could hear the voices of those guests who were pacing to and fro, or standing upon the terrace. Now there came to them the curious, muffled, yet continuous noise produced by a hundred light feet skimming over polished floors—a moment more and they were able to catch glimpses of the dancers themselves. Soon it would be all over, that brief time spent in paradise, which Mr. Gayre knew he should never, while life lasted, forget. Involuntarily, almost, he slackened his already tardy steps, and said,

"Do not walk so fast, Miss Drummond. You are tired."

"Fast!" she repeated; "slow, rather, even for a snail;" at the same time, however, following his example, while she turned a thoughtful dreamy face towards the gleaming lights and the laughing groups, and the flitting figures as they appeared and disappeared within the rooms.

"If you could choose your lot in life," asked the banker, breaking in upon her reverie, "what would it be?"

"You ask a very strange question," said Susan, turning towards him a glance eloquent in its wistful astonishment.

"Do I? And yet one I should imagine easily answered. We all have, or have had, I suppose, our dreams of what we should like life to prove. If some enchanter put it into your power to-night to select your path, where would you have it lie? Across the hill-top or winding among lowly valleys? Should you select to be rich and great, or humble and out of the battle? Perhaps, like Agur, of whom we are told so very little, you would pray for a happy mean?"

"I don't think I should," she replied.

"What would you ask for, then?" he persisted. "Wealth, power, love, genius?"

She shook her head.

"Is it that you will not tell me, or that, never having thought the question out previously, you are unable to decide?"

"I never have thought about the matter before," she said. "Still, I fancy I know what I should most wish to be able to do."

"And that is—?"

"You must not laugh, Mr. Gayre, if I tell you—I could not bear you to laugh."

"On my honour, I won't laugh, no matter how extraordinary your desire may seem."

"I should wish, then—"

"Yes, Miss Drummond?" for she stopped and hesitated.

"To be able to make the best of whatever lot was appointed for me. If I were wise I know I should not ask for riches, or competence, or happiness, or talent, or renown; but simply that I might have strength and wisdom given me to be, not merely content in the state of life assigned but to make a 'good thing of it,' as Sir Geoffrey would say." And for a moment, in the starlight, Mr. Gayre could see a smile wreathe Susan's lips and chase away the grave shadows that had seemed to change the whole expression of her tender lovely face.

For a moment the banker was startled —actually startled. He had long felt the girl's daily life and practice to be a lay sermon; but he was scarcely prepared for such a confession of faith as that involved in the words she uttered. Just at first he did not understand, even dimly, what she meant, and days and weeks and months, and even years, were destined to pass before the man thoroughly comprehended youth in its ignorance may conceive a simple and sublime ideal that shall yet, with tears and struggles, with sorrow and pain, eventually impress something like the image of Divinity upon broken and contrite hearts, or souls worn, weary, and buffeted by the billows of temptation, by the agony of remorse!

Had he only known it, he was standing then under the starlight side by side with his better angel. Yet the world and the things of the world left him without other answer to her words than the question,

"Are you a fatalist, Miss Drummond? Do you believe we cannot even rough-hew the marble of our lives?"

"I believe," she answered, "that as we cannot forecast the events of the next twenty-four hours, as we are unable to tell in the morning what may occur before night, 'free will' resolves itself into whether we shall be good or bad children in our school and playtime. Fact is, Mr. Gayre," added Susan, with a gaiety which had a touch of underlying sadness, "I have been enjoying life too much lately, and so I want to prepare myself to bear the dark days bravely when they come—as come they must."

"You add the Spirit of Prophecy to the Voice of the Preacher, Miss Drummond."

"Thank you for listening to the words of both so gravely," answered Susan; and as she spoke she would have taken her hand from his arm, and turned to enter the house by a glass door opening on a corridor which split the cottage in twain, and gave egress to all the reception and some of the principal bed rooms, had not Mr. Gayre detained her

" Indeed, indeed," he said, " I meant no sarcasm. I feel there is truth underlying your words, though I confess I do not exactly comprehend them. Why should you, in your sunny youth, talk so wisely concerning dark days ? Why should you from whom all true men would keep even the knowledge of sin and trouble, imagine it could ever prove necessary for you to ' make the best of your lot in life ? ' "

" Because I have known sorrow, and am certain I shall know more; besides, Mr. Gayre, even if such a thing were possible, I should not *like* to live a perfectly pros- perous and easy life. One ought to see both sides."

" True daughter of Eve, you want to pluck of the tree of the knowledge of good and evil ! I really cannot recollect ever having heard you take so despondent a view of life before. Is it Mr. Hilderton's

poverty, or Mr. Sudlow's plenty, or this gay
and festive scene, which causes you to
regard existence as so utterly gloomy an
affair ? "

She did not answer for a moment.
Somehow, as he paused and listened, he
felt rather than heard she was catching a
sobbing breath; then just as it seemed he
could contain himself no longer, as if he
must pour forth the full torrent he had so
long restrained, she said, with a little touch
of her usual vivacity,

"There are some people, you know, Mr.
Gayre, in whom the spectacle of a crowd
induces a far greater melancholy than the
sight of a single corpse. Especially if the
corpse has had anything to bequeath. Well,
in a different way that is my case to-night.
I suppose it is only because I am so tired
that I project myself (that is a good word)
to a time when not merely in those now
brilliantly lighted rooms there won't be a

single guest, but when I myself, Susan
Drummond, shall feel

> " Like one who treads alone
>   Some banquet-hall deserted."

Forgive me, Mr. Gayre; ah, I did not
mean to make you gloomy too. I am
going to Mrs. Jubbins; I want to ask her
a favour." And with a smile she left him
at the porch, and crossing the wide hall
made her way to the inner drawing-room,
from which a few days previously had
proceeded the speech that struck Deputy
Pettell dumb. Following close upon her
Mr. Gayre saw the girl glide behind the
easy-chairs and lounges where dowagers sat
fanning themselves, and exchanging weighty
confidences concerning household matters,
and the perfections of their children, till
she reached Mrs. Jubbins, standing near
one of the windows talking to Mr. Brown,
who felt even his great mansion at Walton-
on-Thames shrink into insignificance beside

Lady Merioneth's "little box," into which,
by a mere freak of Fortune, the widow had
walked as "coolly and unconcernedly as if
she were as intimately acquainted with
noblemen's houses as with the old place in
Brunswick Square." For a minute Susan
stood quietly waiting, her face white as her
dress, and a far-off yearning expression in
those soft tender brown eyes the banker
had never seen before. Then suddenly
Mrs. Jubbins turning became aware of her
presence. Whatever Susan's request, it was
evidently granted with pleasure. The hostess
touched the fair cheek with her fan, lin-
geringly, lovingly. Mr. Gayre could have
blessed the buxom Eliza for that graceful
caress. Then as Miss Drummond, threading
her way back as dexterously as she had
come, passed through the archway into the
long drawing-room, where dancing was in
progress, Mrs. Jubbins made some remark
to the Walton-on-Thames Crœsus the banker

knew had kindly reference to his niece's friend.

Still standing by the door, he saw Susan's white dress flitting down the corridor. It went on and on, past the hall, past the dining and morning and billiard rooms, past the library and the state bed-chambers; finally disappearing down a passage at right angles with the main gallery. Through the music, through the tip-tapping of the dancers' feet, through the buzz of conversation, and the clatter of plates, and popping of corks in the supper-room, he heard the closing of a distant door, and Susan Drummond did not again that night bless his sight.

What could have gone wrong? What was the matter with her? He waited and waited for her re-appearance, but waited in vain. All the guests who wished to catch the last train had gone. Weary chaperons were casting stern and reproachful glances at girls who persisted in just one dance

more, one more still; even Mrs. Jubbins'
prosperous face began to show signs of
wear and tear.   Amongst the musicians a
man fell out occasionally to rest.   The
hours had told on the waiters, some of
whom looked limp as to their cravats, and
dishevelled about the head.   Still the young
people went on dancing fresh and gay, as
though the party were just beginning; but
Susan came not, and Mr. Gayre's anxiety
and curiosity concerning what had become
of her grew all the more intense, because
he did not wish to ask any questions concerning the missing guest.

With discontented and cynical eyes he
was looking at his niece as she floated to
the melody of a ravishing waltz round one
of the ball-rooms, pioneered by that capti-
vating sinner Graceless, when one of the
old Bloomsbury set, a contemporary of
Mr. Jubbins, who had scores of times
religiously played out rubber after rubber

of whist in Brunswick Square, accosted him.

"Not dancing, Gayre?" began this individual, who was the human embodiment of snow in harvest; "leaving it for the juniors? You're right—no fool like an old one, you know! Well, and what do you think of all this? Things were different in my day, and in yours too, for that matter, It is enough to make Jubbins turn in his grave. If your wise father had been alive we'd have seen nothing of this sort. He'd have read madam a lecture. There are people here whose names would not be thought much of across a bill-stamp, eh? You've come to look after your niece, I suppose! Handsome girl! doesn't take after your side of the house, at any rate. It is astonishing though, how hard it is to get men to marry beauties. They fight shy of them when it comes to that, and I am sure I don't wonder at it.

" Have you had any supper ? I give you my solemn word I could not get a mouthful fit for any Christian man to eat till a quarter of an hour ago, when I seized the butler and made him bring me a cut of cold beef out of the larder, and a pint of draught ale. I know their draught ale of old. Jubbins always dealt with Flowers, and she keeps up the charter.

" I shall be glad to be at home and in my bed, and I daresay you will, too. It is hard upon you, just when you must be beginning to feel you want rest and quiet, having that girl on your hands. However, Mrs. Jubbins will perhaps help you to get her off. She played her own cards so remarkably well, I daresay she can put your niece up to a thing or two.

" And so it was you looked out this fine place for the widow, eh ? You know the sex ! Give women their way about finery, and fashion, and folly, and you may lead them where you like by the nose. You're a sly dog, Gayre! Not a bad sort of peg this to hang up your hat on for life, though the money that pays the rent was made out of dirty oil. You're a sly dog!"

Having emphasised which pleasant utterance with an evil chuckle and a dig in the ribs, the old friend of the family took himself off, leaving Mr. Gayre speechless with indignation.

" You look as if you had lost a shilling, and not found even sixpence," said Sir Geoffrey, at this juncture taking up a position beside his brother-in-law. The Baronet was just beginning really to enjoy the evening. He had drunk himself sober, if such an apparent paradox is intelligible. It was a way Sir Geoffrey had, or rather, as he frequently explained, a way his constitution had. At the first start, when he began his libations—if that, indeed, could be said ever to begin which was only suspended by sleep—strong liquors did apparently produce an effect faintly simulating intoxication ; but as time went on, these evidences of a weak brain disappeared totally.

" Fact is," said Sir Geoffrey, " drink steadies me." He spoke of it as a sea-faring person might of ballast. He did not roll when he had his due complement aboard, and he was extremely ingenious in accounting for the extraordinary pheno-menon, that the more champagne, or brandy, or " whatever was going " he swallowed, the soberer he became.

" It is like this, you know," he declared : " every family, I take it, must, in the course of a few generations, drink a certain amount ; I daresay statistics could get at the amount. Well, then, don't you see, if three or four of the lot fail to take their fair share, there must at last come some poor devil of a scapegoat like myself, who has to drink for the lot. I call it hard, deuced hard! I am sure, even on the score of expense, I'd like to live on tea and lemonade; but Lord! when you've a constitution like mine to deal with, what are you to do?" A question so abstruse and so impossible to answer, that nobody tried to grapple with the difficulty presented by the singular nature of Sir Geoffrey's internal arrangements.

In a state then of steadiness and comprehension a teetotaller might have envied, Sir Geoffrey, seeing Mr. Gayre part company with the Bloomsbury friend, sauntered across and made that remark anent the banker's shilling and sixpence expression of face.

Desirous, no doubt, of emulating the little busy bee, Sir Geoffrey lounged about the rooms, affably entering into conversation with utter strangers, and, indeed, helping to do the honours for Mrs. Jubbins, as he might had Lady Chelston gone to a better world, and the widow and himself been engaged. Now and then, in this chance ride across country, he met with a crushing retort or a nasty fall ; and from experience, he knew pretty well what ' the crusty, white-haired, and red-nosed old party had been saying to Gayre.' "

" Deuced mixed lot this," he observed, with a solemn shake of his knowing head. " I thought I'd seen a thing or two during the course of a life which has not been wholly spent in the quiet country ; but hang me if I ever could have imagined such a set out as this ! "

" It must, indeed, seem a change to you to find yourself among so many solvent and respectable people," retorted Mr. Gayre, who was glad to vent his irritation on any one.

" That's right, pass the blow round, my lad ! It does not hurt me," said the

Baronet. "Solvent?" he went on, looking about him, "no doubt of that; but respectable? h'm—m—m! I notice some folks here who, unless I am greatly out in my reckoning, have sailed uncommonly close to the wind. But then *their* haul was ten thousands, or hundreds of thousands, which makes all the difference, Gayre, all the difference."

"The whole thing is a confounded bore," remarked his brother-in-law, who did not feel inclined at that moment to take up the cudgels for trade morality.

"Peggy's having the fun of the fair," observed that young lady's parent. "I don't think she has sat out one dance, and I have seen her send away would-be partners by the dozen. Lord, what a sly jade it is! How does she do it? Just a modest downcast look, and an uplifted appealing look, or the slightest turn of the shoulders, or an indolent movement of her fan, and she has all the men about her. I have been watching her, and wondering. It is extraordinary. That sort of thing would not attract me; but it seems to suit other people. It is not my style."

"No, I don't think it is," agreed Mr. Gayre, who knew too well the type of frisky and frolicsome young lady the Baronet delighted in.

"But she's a splendid girl," proceeded Sir Geoffrey; "just look at her now. Faith, in that dress—I wonder how much the bill for it will tot up to?—she resembles nothing except some rare tropical bird. Gad! what a splendid colour she has to-night, just like the inner leaves of a damask rose! And her feet—there is not a woman in the room has such a foot and ankle; all the Chelstons had good feet. Poor Margaret had pretty feet too, though a trifle low in the instep. Seriously now, Gayre, don't you think it's a thousand pities Peggy should be thrown away on mere wealth? She'd make a capital countess, and even as a duchess she would only be the right thing in the right place."

"Well, if you know any stray earl or duke in want of a wife, you might mention the matter to him," suggested Mr. Gayre.

"I declare the more I see of Peggy the less I feel I can bear the notion of her being wasted on such a fellow as Sudlow. Why, he's a perfect cad, and a stick in addition. He can't skate, and he can't ride, and he can't dance, and he can't shoot; what the deuce can he do?"

"Take care of his money," answered the banker; "and all I hope is he may give her a chance of helping him to take care of it also."

"Well, I suppose we must make the best of a bad business," said Sir Geoffrey, with religious resignation; "I am sure I try to do so. I gave her a hint or two before we came here; I told her she must not neglect her opportunities. The worst of her is she's such a flirt, always was, always will be; I don't mean in any dangerous way—bless you, no! She'll take good care to get into no harm; I could trust Peg anywhere, trust her as I could myself;" which, indeed, was saying so little for the charming Peggy's discretion, that Mr. Gayre had to turn away his face and hide a smile. "I wish she'd some female relations up in all that sort of thing," proceeded Sir Geoffrey, with an easy wave of his hand, indicating that he meant the art of securing eligible husbands, "just to give her a chance; she wants training. Heavens! well schooled, she might marry whom she pleased. It's no use thinking of what's past; but if her poor mother—"

At which juncture the Baronet stopped and sighed, and shook his head and sighed again.

"Out of the fulness of your own abundant experience," suggested Mr. Gayre, "don't you think you might advise your daughter for her good—tell her how to set about the great sport of hunting men?"

"No, my dear fellow," answered the Baronet, who, if he imagined his brother-in-law was sneering at him, took care not to seem cognisant of the fact. "In the first place, to be truly successful, it should be pursued as a business, not a sport; and in the next, only a woman can really teach a woman how to deal with the other sex. If a man, now—yourself, for instance—stood in want of a few tips, couldn't I give them? and wouldn't I, with pleasure? But, bless my soul, your running is all straight enough. Here are you, and there's the

widow; you've only to say 'Come,' and
she'll come fast enough, and why the
deuce you don't say it baffles me."

"I must request, Sir Geoffrey—"

"O yes, I know all about that; but re-
quests don't alter cases, and though you
may insist on people shutting their mouths,
you can't compel them to close their eyes.
Well, she's as pleasant and hospitable a
woman as I'd ever desire to meet, and I
will say she, or somebody for her, has a
judgment in the matter of wine I wish
were universal. You'll weed out a lot of
these people, no doubt," and he nodded
towards the room where what he called
the "old fogies" were "playing at company."
"Poor soul, she knows no better; but you'll
teach her, Gayre—you'll teach her; and—
she'll make an apt pupil;" having delivered
which last opinion, the Baronet was turning away, probably to quite assure his
mind as to whether Mrs. Jubbins' brandy

was as good as her hock, when, inspired
by a fresh idea, he paused to ask,

"By-the-bye, where's Susan? I haven't
seen the little baggage for ages. She
looked a bit bleached, I thought, a while
ago; wonder where she's got to? There's
Lal Hilderton, face, as usual, black as
a thunder-cloud. No doubt he knows.
Hilderton — Lal — come here, can't you !
Where's Susan ?"

"Haven't seen her for an hour or more."

"Where the deuce can she be ? " remarked Sir Geoffrey. "How are you
going to get back to your 'diggins'
to-night, Lal ? "

"Irish tandem," was the curt reply.

"Come and have something, then, to
give your horses spirit for the journey,"
said the Baronet, taking the young man's
reluctant arm, and leading him tenderly
towards the supper-room.

Where was Susan? where could she be?

Miss Chelston did not know; for, pausing with Mr. Graceless close to where Mr. Gayre stood, she propounded the very question to her uncle he was longing to hear answered by some one.

" She is not going back to town to-night.," said Mrs. Jubbins, appearing at the moment Margaret was prettily expressing her wonder and astonishment. " She is tired ; she has been doing too much, and I've sent her to bed."

For a second Miss Chelston looked at the speaker with incredulous surprise; then, seeing the hostess was not jesting, she pressed her fan against her chin, puckered her forehead, raised her eyebrows, murmured, " I am *so* sorry," and next moment the maize dress, with its splashes of colour, was whirling amongst the dancers, a dream of beauty and delight.

CHAPTER II.

ON THE WAY HOME.

"POOR Susan! poor, dear, kind, tiresome Susan!" lamented Miss Chelston. "These are the sort of things she always would do. Almost kill herself to please people who scarcely considered it worth their while to say thank you; always ready to wear herself out for anybody."

"I call the whole proceeding extremely silly, to say the least of it," observed Mr. Sudlow.

"Do you?" said Mr. Gayre.

"Yes, I do," retorted Mr. Sudlow, in a tone intended to convince young Graceless he was out of the banker's leading-strings at last.

"And what," said Mr. Gayre, "should you call the proceeding, if you said the most of it?"

"That's a question I decline to answer," answered the gentleman tersely styled "the cad" by Sir Geoffrey; hearing which valiant reply, Mr. Graceless burst out laughing.

They were all driving back to London together—Miss Chelston, Messieurs Sudlow, Graceless, and Gayre—with Sir Geoffrey on the box; three of the party in extremely bad temper, and one not too well pleased at finding himself booked as inside passenger for a fourteen miles' journey, unable to smoke, and thrown on the companionship of two men and a girl, with none of whom he had an idea in common.

As for Miss Chelston, she felt most truly it was the day after the fair. Such triumph as she had compassed was over, and her

triumph could not, in such an assemblage,
be considered great. Amid better surroundings, her beauty, her figure, her grace, her
manner, her voice, must have placed her on
a high rung of the social ladder; but upon
the City magnates she was thrown away.
The old men regarded her merely as a good-
looking girl without a fortune, who ,no
doubt, knew more about spending money
than saving it; while their sons felt somewhat shy of a Baronet's daughter whose
ways and looks and tones seemed different
from the ways, looks, and tones of belles
renowned in civic circles. She was the right
thing among the wrong set of people. She
had striven her best to please; she had
smiled on the sons of prospective Lord
Mayors; she had, in her quiet undemonstra-
tive way, flirted with wealthy young stock-
brokers and rising junior partners in great
City houses; she had borne herself meekly
towards large and portly mammas, and

refrained from looking amazed at the
doings of Cockney heiresses; and yet,
when the sum of the day and evening
was told, she felt her talents had not
returned her even fair interest. If Mrs.
Jubbins' party represented the best her
uncle could do for her socially, bad indeed
was the best. She had only really felt
herself in a proper element while dancing
with one or other of the "fellows" Sir
Geoffrey offered as his graceful contribution
to the Chislehurst festivities; and as she
knew too well what they were, and what
they had, and that each of them was
looking out for a flat, or an heiress, or
both, on his own account, it goes without
saying that even in the delicious curves
of that final waltz with Mr. Graceless
she was perfectly well aware nothing could
ever come of such an acquaintance, save,
perhaps, if hereafter she got into a safe
and unexceptionable clique, a little regret

at ever having known so polished and presentable a blackleg.

With the result of the day's proceedings Mr. Gayre felt, if possible, more dissatisfied than his niece. He had arrived at the conclusion that he did not understand Susan in the least; that she would require more careful management than he anticipated; that below her sweet amiability and charming frankness there lay a depth of character and a power of will, both of which it might be necessary to gauge and to conciliate. Time was when he thought he knew her thoroughly; day by day it was dawning upon him he really knew her less. The old qualities which had so captivated him on first acquaintance remained unchanged, but fresh and unexpected qualities were, in addition, constantly appearing. She was like a garden which a man first values for the sake of a few simple and homely flowers almost gone out of fashion, and behold, as the days go by, other plants thrust their tender leaves above ground, and he is kept in a constant state of uncertainty as to the manner of blossom which shall next appear.

As an acquaintance, even as a friend, perhaps she had drawn nearer to him; but as a lover, no. Mr. Gayre was too sensible a man, far too well learned in the lore of a world which contains both men and women, to blind himself to facts. Before he knew Susan Drummond he would have laid it down as a general proposition that all women were enigmas. Since he had known Susan he would have done battle on the point that he was acquainted with one woman who wore her heart on her sleeve; but now—now—now—Mr. Gayre could not exactly tell what to think. Leaning back in his corner, he felt sorely tempted to speedily put his fortune to the test, and "maybe," he considered, "lose it all."

O sweet Susan, sleeping that night among the Chislehurst woods, dreaming your maiden dreams in the house where noble lovers had kissed and been blessed, had wept and been parted till eternity, how was it possible for you to imagine a middle-aged man's heart was being rent because he failed to read aright your simple sincerity?

He felt wild to know his hands held no prize the girl seemed to account of value. Wealth, rank, jewels, pleasure, idleness—the five curses and snares of womanhood—she held, apparently, of no worth whatever. What did her youth long for, his middle age could give? Now he was beginning to understand her better, he saw Susan was prepared to sit down to the feast of life with a purpose of abstinence for which he could find no possible reason. She loved riding, dancing, society, travelling. Even to the simplest excursion she brought a zest and a sunshine he had never seen equalled. Yet he fully understood she expected at some not remote day to resign all chance of such pleasures, and live quietly at Enfield with her aunt.

"I mean to grapple with the mysteries of farming next year," she said to Mr. Gayre one day. "I don't think I could serve my country better than in trying to solve the problem of how to make land pay. Aunt cannot. I see where she goes wrong; but that is quite another matter from seeing how I am to go right."

"I will come over and help you," offered Sir Geoffrey. "I know all about farming. If my tenants would only have followed my advice I need never have left Chelston. Now they have got another landlord they wish, I'll be bound, they had considered me a little more. Do you remember, Susan, the talks your uncle and I used to have about cropping and how he broke up the ten-acre lot, and sowed flax entirely on my advice?"

ON THE WAY HOME.

"Very well indeed," answered Susan, demurely. She had good reason for remembering the circumstance, since, owing to dry soil and the utter impossibility of irrigation, the result proved a dead failure.

"I'll only make one stipulation," proceeded the irrepressible Baronet—"that you lay in a cask of beer. I ask nothing more expensive. Hang it, there never was a man with simpler tastes! But water! and New River water, too! Fugh!" and Sir Geoffrey drew down the corners of his mouth—he could not turn up his nose, because it was aquiline—and pulled a grimace expressive of the most intense disgust.

"I must talk to my aunt about the ale," said Susan.

"Come, you don't mean to say, my girl, you are going to turn yourself out to grass like Nebuchadnezzar, and drink nothing stronger than water, as if you were a cow or a dog? Why, even a horse knows better. Gad! I wouldn't keep a brute that refused honest liquor."

Susan and Mr. Gayre simultaneously broke into a peal of laughter.

"I am growing rather in love with teetotalism," said the former. "It is cheap and healthful."

"The cheapness I admit, but the health I deny," retorted the Baronet. "I only know one fellow who denies his blood natural nourishment, and he's covered with as many boils and blains as Job; only Job got cured, and he never will. Serve him right, too."

Once, when opportunity offered, Mr. Gayre hazarded an inquiry to Sir Geoffrey concerning the why and the wherefore of Miss Drummond's conviction that she would have to content herself with a humdrum existence and very modest surroundings, and though the answer he received seemed to him scarcely satisfactory, it was at least plausible.

" Susan's a confoundedly sensible sort of a girl," said the Baronet. " Always was. Bless you, I used to call her little old woman when she wasn't more than eight hands high. She ought to have been a big heiress, a fine haul for some lucky young fellow, but the house in which her father left his money went smash, and she never got a penny out of the wreck but a beggarly two thousand pounds. Her uncle Drummond was a man who could not save a farthing—most extravagant old dog ; so when he died, and the son came into the estate, there was poor Susan adrift with about sixty pounds a year, and no near relation except the ancient party at Enfield. Many a girl would have broken her heart ; but that's not Susan's way. She'll make the best of a bad busi-ness, and when that young Arbery's gone

back to the Antipodes take sole management."

"Yes, I understand all that," replied the
banker; "but why should she speak as
if she was going totally out of society?
Now, she comes here, for instance; why
should she imply she will not be able to
continue to do so?"

"Well, for two reasons, I suppose: one,
I don't fancy the aunt will care to be
left alone; another, Susan knows Peggy
must marry; and she's not so blind as
to imagine my good daughter would care
for her as a constant or even occasional
inmate. Peg's jealous of her, that's the
truth. Besides, Susan's not grand enough,
or rich enough, or dressy enough, or
stuck up enough to please her ladyship.
Yes, you may stare, but though Peggy's
my own child, I can see her faults. I
don't know where she gets them, upon
my soul, I don't—not from me; and as

for her poor mother, if your sister hadn't much wit, at any rate she was a loving clinging creature. You mayn't believe it, Gayre, but I've often felt very sorry for Margaret. Most men would only think of themselves, but, thank Heaven, that's not my way;" and Sir Geoffrey paused, either because he was stricken dumb with the contemplation of his own merits, or because he wished to give his brother-in-law time to recover from the astonishment he believed such unparalleled magnanimity might well excite.

Whatever his emotions, Mr. Gayre controlled them admirably.

"Still, I fail to comprehend Miss Drummond," he persisted. "Most girls look forward to marriage as an end to all difficulty, the beginning of a brilliant and delightful existence. Why should she not feel certain that a husband as rich and handsome as Cinderella's prince will one day cross her path?"

"Because, as I told you before, Susan is as wise as Solomon. She knows well enough it is not so easy to pick up a rich husband; if it were, clever though she is, she is not the sort of girl to hook a big fish. Besides, her own sense must tell her that if Peggy, a baronet's daughter and so forth, hangs fire, she has not much chance of going off to any good purpose. Fact is," went on Sir Geoffrey, shaking his remarkable head till his hat actually quivered, "men can't afford to marry nowadays, unless the lady brings something in her hand, and something considerable too. There's no end to the expenses of a married man. They begin with the engagement ring, and they don't end when he is screwed down in his coffin. It's no joking matter, I can tell you. Men don't care a straw, at this date of the world, what a

girl is; what they want to be told is what
she has. For himself, a man is always
worth his own value in the matrimonial
market, but a woman isn't; there's such a
deuce of a lot of them!"

Mr. Gayre was thinking of these utterances, and many more, as they drove
steadily on through the chill twilight of
that summer's night, when suddenly the
carriage stopped, and Sir Geoffrey shouted
to some one they had just passed, " Jump
up, man; we'll make room for you on the
box; you've done enough for glory; come
along!"

"Thank you, I'd rather walk," answered
a sulky voice, which belonged to Lionel
Hilderton, and none other.

> "With my left leg for leader,
> And right leg for wheeler,
> I'll distance all racers, says Pat.
> Hoo-roo!
> I'll distance all racers, says Pat."

chanted the Baronet. " Don't be a fool,

Lal," he added, in sober prose. "It's thirteen miles from here to Camden Town, if it's a step. If you have no mercy on yourself, have some on your boots!"

Even Susan Drummond could scarce have found an apology for the reply to Sir Geoffrey's genial speech, which though muttered, was distinctly audible to every person in the carriage.

"Have your own bad way, then, my friend," retorted the Baronet; "I'll not baulk you. Walk and be—— !"

"Poor Mr. Hilderton!" exlaimed Miss Chelston as they drove on.

"Lovely woman!" commented Mr. Sudlow.

"Yes, it's what we are all bound to go through," said Mr. Gayre, who, having now a perfect knowledge of the name of that lovely woman, derived the keenest enjoyment from Mr. Sudlow's remark.

"And the most delightful part of the business is, that by this time next year he will be thinking what a special Providence it was that she refused to smile on him," capped young Graceless.

" I hope you like *that*, my lady," thought Mr. Gayre, striving in vain to catch a glimpse of his niece's face.

Almost in silence the dreary journey was got through somehow. If there ever had been a time when Mr. Graceless enjoyed the society of a respectable woman it was long past; and after the utterance of a few commonplace phrases, he began to think what a nuisance it was he could not smoke, to wonder whether the old City " duffer" would stand to the bargain made with Sir Geoffrey, how much the Baronet would expect for his share of the spoil; and finally, exhausted by these mental labours, he fell asleep, for doing which he afterwards apologised by explaining he had " made a long day," viz. thirty-four hours, not having gone to bed at all on the night preceding Mrs. Jubbins' party.

As for Mr. Sudlow, he was in a white heat of rage at the presence of this interloper. He felt jealous, envious, disappointed. Although Miss Chelston had, during the early part of the day, shown him a good deal of favour, when once dancing commenced he found himself put somehow out of court. Graceless, without a sovereign in his pocket, was, in a ball-room, a greater man than Mr. Sudlow; and not merely Graceless, but all the guests introduced by Sir Geoffrey.

"They dance like *seraphs!*" said one gushing young lady to the disgusted Dives, who did not dance like anything on earth or in heaven except like himself, who walked through a quadrille with the solemn grace of a poker, and extracted, apparently, a vast deal less pleasure out of a wild galop than he would have done from a religious procession.

"He likes no concert where he can't play first fiddle," said the Baronet, afterwards summing him up; and as he certainly did not do that at The Warren, it goes without saying Mr. Sudlow's enjoyment of the evening's proceedings was not of an ecstatic character.

On and still on, weary mile after weary mile; the gray dawn came raw and miserable; objects by the wayside began to be visible, and it was with a jaded feeling of relief the revellers found themselves at last jolting over the London stones. How hard and cold the river looked in the first beams of the morning sun! What a blessed sight the Houses of Parliament seemed, holding as it did an assurance Middlesex was reached once more! On and still on. What an endless distance they appeared to have driven! How cramped and stiff they felt! How exasperatingly maddening Sir Geoffrey's cheery and wide-awake tones sounded, as he hailed his brother-in-law to ask,

"Shall we go round by Wimpole Street, Gayre? Drop you at your door with pleasure."

"Certainly not," answered Mr. Gayre; "we will get out here;" and, suiting his action to his word, he opened the carriage-door and stepped out, leaving Mr. Sudlow to follow his good example.

"I'll take your place now," said the Baronet, jumping down from the box. "It's getting a bit chilly. No, Graceless, keep where you are; we'll find you a sofa, never fear. Hope you'll be none the worse, Mr. Sudlow; by-by, Gayre!" and Sir Geoffrey put up the window, and remarked to all whom the intelligence might concern that it was deucedly cold.

"What does he mean by it?" was the

astounding question Mr. Sudlow put to his companion as the carriage rolled away.

"What does who mean by what?" asked Mr. Gayre, in amazement.

"Your brother-in-law! What does he mean by taking that fellow Graceless to his house and talking about finding him a sofa?"

"Are you mad, Mr. Sudlow?" said the banker, "Do you suppose Sir Geoffrey Chelston cannot ask any one he likes to his house without your permission?"

"He has no business to allow his daughter to associate with such a man"

"May I inquire by what right you presume to dictate with whom his daughter shall associate? What is Miss Chelston to you, that you should even express an opinion on the subject? You are tired and a little irritable, Mr. Sudlow; so I will only say, that it seems to me you have of late, more than once, strangely forgotten yourself!"

CHAPTER III.

SIR GEOFFREY'S TACTICS.

"LEAVE me to deal with the fellow, Gayre," said Sir Geoffrey cheerfully." "You are not fit for the task. In your own way you are confoundedly clever —no doubt of that; but aptitude for business is one thing—gad, I wish I wasn't such a fool about figures and money!—and a knowledge of human nature another. You made a mistake with your friend— one you would not have caught your simple brother-in-law committing. He never ought to have gone with us to Mrs. Jubbins— never. He thinks now Peggy and myself are no better than her lot, and that *he is as good as we are.* He thought great guns of you once; now he knows your 'native heath' is much the same as his own—" and as the Baronet left his sentence thus unfinished, in order to light a fresh cigar, Mr. Gayre felt the pause which ensued more explicit and humiliating than any words could have proved.

It was three days after the party at The Warren. Mrs. Jubbins had been discussed, re-discussed, praised, criticised, disparaged, blamed; and now there was nothing left for the majority of her guests to do save call and see whether "the Earl of Merioneth's house" seemed as grand a place when viewed in cold blood as it had done while filled with visitors who walked through the rooms to the strains of music and the popping of champagne corks. Things during that three days had not been going pleasantly with Mr. Gayre; on the contrary, when he went to Chislehurst, ostensibly to inquire how Mrs. Jubbins felt after her exertions, he found Miss Drummond was walking through the woods, accompanied by Mr. Hilderton. The widow told him this fact with a look of mournful significance, and he really felt too much dispirited to inform the lady he was satisfied his niece, and not her friend, had won the poor prize of a struggling and sulky artist's heart. No, many a man was caught on the rebound, and he did not know, he could not be sure. After all, the girl might scarcely understand her own mind ; possibly she mistook the actual state of her feelings. This sisterly sort of intimacy, this familiar intercourse, was dangerous—very.

Supposing Susan were Mrs. Gayre, would he allow, would he tolerate it? Certainly, Mr. Gayre decided, he would do nothing of the kind. It was all very well to talk, but Lal was not her brother; worse still, he was disgustingly handsome—and young. Yes, just the lover a girl might fancy ;

and Susan was only a girl, and the com-
mon-sense view of the matter must be considered the right sense. The whole thing
was unusual and incorrect. He thought
he would drop a word of warning ; but,
somehow, when the culprits appeared, he
found it would be very hard to make
Miss Drummond understand the full enor-
mity of which she had been guilty, and
decided that to lecture her on the subject of " propriety " would be like dis-
coursing to a child concerning those sins
which it is the endeavour of older persons, who have eaten of the tree of the
knowledge of good and evil, to keep
hidden from its innocence.

At dinner, to which meal Mr. Gayre
stopped, for Mrs. Jubbins would take no
denial, Susan was charming ; less gay than
formerly, perhaps a little sad, certainly
most sweet. She had been teaching Ida
to ride, and caused some laughter by

an account of that young lady's mis-
haps.

"I don't know what in the world we
are to do without her, Mr. Gayre," said
Mrs. Jubbins, referring to Susan, not her
daughter; "we shall feel lost."

"When is the parting to take place?"
asked the banker, who felt delighted to
hear Miss Drummond's sojourn at Chislehurst was soon to be ended.

"I am going to Enfield to-morrow," said
Susan.

"*To Enfield!*" repeated Mr. Gayre; "not
to North Bank?"

"I have written to tell Maggie I cannot
return there just at present."

"So we shall *all* have to go into mourn-
ing," said the banker; at which remark
Lal Hilderton scowled. He thought this
rich man was sneering at his old friend.

The next check Mr. Gayre met was
received from the artist. In the most

courteous manner possible he asked Mr. Hilderton to paint Miss Chelston's portrait, and was met with a flat refusal.

"I don't intend to paint any more portraits," declared Lal, with rude directness.

Susan looked at him reproachfully and sighed. Mr. Gayre saw the look and heard the sigh.

"It breaks my heart to think of her being tied to such a bear," said Mrs. Jubbins afterwards.

"Why did you ask him here?" inquired the banker.

"I did not ask him. He came, and I could not well tell him to go. Of course he will not come when she is gone;" which was very poor comfort for the middle-aged lover.

Calling the following afternoon at North Bank, in hopes of hearing why Susan had decided on returning to Enfield, and when she might be again expected in

Mr. Moreby's villa, he found Mr. Sudlow partaking of afternoon tea, and was unpleasantly struck by a change in his manner, rather to be felt than defined. They had not met since the morning when Mr. Gayre administered what he meant for a crushing rebuke, and the banker was certainly not prepared to find this former disciple had cut his leading-strings, and was walking quite independently about the world, " showing his d——d cloven foot," said Sir Geoffrey.

Few things could have discomposed Mr. Gayre to an equal extent. Hitherto Mr. Sudlow had looked up to him, adopted his views, being guided by his advice, received his admonitions modestly and in a good spirit, as if he knew they proceeded from one having authority; but now all that was changed. He ventured to disagree with the banker, not once or twice, but many times; he spoke more familiarly to Sir

Geoffrey than young Graceless would have done ; and only the beautiful coldness and propriety of Miss Chelston's demeanour prevented his addressing that young lady " as though she was some girl standing behind a counter, by Heaven!" declared the Baronet, talking " the cad " over after his departure.

Much exercised about the change which seemed to him to have been wrought so suddenly, Mr. Gayre told Sir Geoffrey that remark concerning young Graceless, and delicately hinted it was not impossible some of those rumours the best of men are not always able to escape, had reached Mr. Sudlow's ears.

" It is not that," answered the Baronet, " I don't pretend to be better than my neighbours. No one can say I have ever set myself up as a paragon of virtue. I admit I have faults; who is without them? Even you, Gayre, are not immaculate, I'll be bound. As for myself, I am too easy, too frank, too trustful, too willing to forgive, too ready to be duped. But it's nothing he has heard about *me* that has caused this transformation. Your friend Sudlow needs taking down a peg; his comb wants cutting, and I'll cut it. Leave me to deal with the fellow."

And then the credulous Baronet, who wore his heart on his sleeve for all the daws he came in contact with to peck at, delivered himself of that pleasant sentence which annoyed Mr. Gayre more than he would have cared to acknowledge.

Sir Geoffrey had an absolute genius for "finding out the raw," and knew there was nothing under heaven that hurt Nicholas Gayre's vanity more keenly than associating him with the old Brunswick Square "set."

Resolutely the banker had for years held himself aloof from his father's con-

nections. In the City he was considered
proud, exclusive, and a genuine "West-
ender." At the West End, among acquain-
tances made during those blessed days
when he served the Queen and never
thought of Lombard Street save as a sort
of gold mine, he was known as an officer
who had won distinction and a banker
who was "rolling in money;" while both
in the City and at the West End people
held him to be exceptionally respectable.
And now, merely for the sake of a girl's
brown eyes, he had voluntarily let himself
drift into close companionship with one of
the most disreputable men in England—
gone to a party at which, a year before,
he would not have been seen for any consideration; where dreadful people, who
were "merely rich" felt themselves at
liberty to call him "Gayre," and address
him in a "hail-fellow-well-met" manner in-
expressibly galling; and, as if this was not

sufficiently mortifying, on the top of all came Sir Geoffrey's statement, which *he knew to be true*, that Mr. Sudlow now believed socially his former Mentor stood very little higher than himself.

"It is always best to look matters straight in the face," proceeded Sir Geoffrey, when he had got his cigar well alight. "There's Peggy to be married, and Sudlow's the only man who has turned up we can marry her to. I hate the fellow, but what am I to do? Of course, I must not let my own likes or dislikes interfere when the girl's happiness is at stake. It's a pity I can't find a husband for her in a decent rank of life; but it is no use fretting about that now. Well, the next thing to be done is—get the man up to the point. I don't intend to have him dangling about here, wasting all our time and trying my temper. You wouldn't believe what a confounded nuisance he is.

Why, I have often to stop in, and lose perhaps the chance of some good thing, because he does not know when to go. It's all very well for him, but we're no further forward than we were last June. I can't bear such dawdling. Gad! the fellow ought to snap at the chance of marrying a Baronet's daughter."

"Apparently he is in no hurry to 'snap,'" said Mr. Gayre, with ill-natured frankness.

"He will be in a hurry before he is much older, or I'll know the reason why," remarked Sir Geoffrey, "which brings me back to the point I started from. It is quite evident, Gayre, that under your management the matter makes no progress. Now I am going to take the conduct of affairs. I don't ask your help because I would rather play my game alone. Fact is," finished the Baronet, "the beggar must be brought to book, for I can't hold on in this way much longer. If I had not been pretty lucky the ball must have stopped rolling weeks ago; and I feel it deucedly provoking for so much of my hard-earned money (no man knows how hard I work) to go in keeping up this house. Were I alone, any attic at a few shillings a week would serve my turn. Besides, I have heard a word drop that young Moreby's mamma has found a wife for him; and if such is the case, you'll see this place will be sold, and then what's to become of poor Peggy? Mark my words—this place will be in the market ere long; you know how right all my intuitions are;" and Sir Geoffrey shook his head with the air of a man who believed there was not a cranny or crack in it unfilled by wisdom.

He had good reason, at any rate, for his belief concerning Mr. Moreby's villa, since the "word dropped" assumed the shape of a letter from Mrs. Moreby's lawyer containing a plain intimation that the sooner he could find another residence the better his client would be pleased.

Except in that trifling matter of paying ready money, or indeed any money at all, no one could complain of undue delay on the part of Sir Geoffrey. Were a horse to be bought or sold, a bet to be laid, a flat to be fleeced, or any other little business of pleasure or profit in hand, the Baronet was "up to time;" and most certainly now he had decided "some steps must be taken about poor Peggy," he did not mean to let grass grow under his feet.

Accordingly next time Mr. Sudlow called, as of late he had got into the habit of doing, unaccompanied by his former friend and Mentor, he found the drawing-room unoccupied, and not the slightest sign of afternoon tea. On the contrary, the gipsy table, which might be regarded as the basis of operations, was put tidily away in one corner of the apartment; the chairs stood also in orthodox positions, and the stands and vases were destitute of flowers.

Mr. Sudlow stared about him bewildered. He had never before imagined the prettiest room in young Mr. Moreby's villa could look so cold and formal. The afternoon also was dull and depressing. No sunshine streamed across the tiny garden, and no fragrant logs burnt in the grate. "Logs are deuced useful sort of things," Sir Geoffrey was in the habit of sententiously remarking.

On that especial day, however, at five o'clock P.M., affairs were chilling in the extreme; and as he stood by the window Mr. Sudlow shivered.

"Bah! what a place this must be in the winter," he considered, "with all that water flowing at the rate of about an inch an hour down below there!"

"How de-do?" said the Baronet, appearing at this point in Mr. Sudlow's meditations, and greeting his daughter's admirer with friendly familiarity and two extended fingers. "Bit raw, ain't it? Come into the next room—fire there; like a fire myself all the year round;" with which statement Sir Geoffrey conducted Mr. Sudlow into the adjoining apartment, where that gentleman found blazing logs and a strong smell of stimulants.

"I suppose we must consider the best of the weather's over now," remarked the host as he threw on another billet.

Mr. Sudlow ventured to hope a fine day or two might still be expected, but Sir Geoffrey would not listen to the suggestion. "We're in September now," he said, "and, faith! winter will be upon us before we can turn round."

After that there ensued a pause. Sir Geoffrey was able, as a rule, to maintain a good even stream of talk, but neither man could be described as a brilliant conversationalist.

"What will you take, Sudlow?" asked the Baronet, inspired by a happy idea, sauntering towards the sideboard as he spoke.

Mr. Sudlow thanked Sir Geoffrey, but declined to take anything.

"It's a beast of a day," said Sir Geoffrey, "'pon my soul it is; worse than if it was raining. Have something, man; I am sure you need picking up; I know I do."

Firmly Mr. Sudlow, or, as the Baronet sometimes loved to describe him, that good young sneak, resisted the temptations and declined the blandishments of his ladye-love's papa. "I never touch wine between meals," he said, repeating a statement Sir Geoffrey had heard before at least fifty times.

"Gad, I envy you; I only wish I could do without it," answered the Baronet; and to prove how imperatively necessary he found it to "pick himself up," he forthwith poured out and swallowed a tumbler of champagne, laced with what he called a mere touch of brandy.

Mr. Sudlow looked on during this performance, but spoke never a word; indeed, what word could he have spoken?

"I feel a new man," said Sir Geoffrey, in that capacity strolling back to the hearth and critically scanning the last log he had thrown on. "Do—take even a glass of sherry, Sudlow."

But Sudlow only shook his head.

"Deuced chilly, I call it," went on the Baronet, settling himself in the depths of an armchair and stretching out his long legs towards the fire. "Well, and what mischief have you been up to since I saw you last?"

"Not much," answered the lively suitor, who detested Sir Geoffrey's jokes, and yet did not well know how to take offence at them. "How is Miss Chelston?"

"O, she's all right," was the reply—"packing."

"Packing!" repeated Mr. Sudlow.

"Yes; of late days she's had unfortunately to manage without a maid, poor girl; so she's doing the best she can, with the help of Mrs. Lavender. They've been at it all day; but I'm afraid to inquire progress."

"Is Miss Chelston, then—"

"She's going out of town," finished the Baronet, with kindly consideration; "and, faith, I'm very glad she is, though I don't exactly know what I am to do here all by myself—you'll take pity upon me, and look in often, won't you?—for the girl has been too long cooped up, losing all her colour, and so forth."

"Is she likely to remain away for any length of time?" asked Mr. Sudlow.

"Can't tell, I'm sure, what she'll do when

she gets among her friends—go the round of
them, I suppose. I'll not bid her come back
to North Bank, you may be sure, while she
keeps well and is enjoying herself elsewhere.
In the length and breadth of England I
suppose there is not so unselfish a father
as myself."

Sudlow murmured some remark under
his breath, which Sir Geoffrey chose to
accept as complimentary; for, after repeating his statement in different and more com-
prehensive terms—viz., that when another
person's interests were to be considered, he
never thought of " Geoffrey Chelston "—he
remained for a short time looking at the
fire with a pensive and satisfied expression
of countenance.

With more courage than might have been
expected under the circumstances, Mr. Sudlow essayed a few commonplace observa-
tions; to all of which Sir Geoffrey replied
heartily, yet in a manner which suggested

to the visitor that his mind was wandering elsewhere.

"Is there any chance of my having the pleasure of seeing Miss Chelston this afternoon?" ventured the lover at last.

The Baronet laughed.

"My good fellow," he said, "it would be 'as much as my place is worth' to ask such a thing. My daughter can't endure to be seen unless she's in parade dress, every bow and brooch and hairpin in its proper place. Funny girl! Now she's in her dressing-gown I wouldn't like to beg for a two minutes' interview myself."

"I did not mean to intrude, of course; I only wished—but perhaps you will kindly tell Miss Chelston I trust she may have an 'extremely pleasant journey.'"

"I don't know much about the journey," answered Sir Geoffrey; "but she's certain to have a good time when she gets to the end of it. Much obliged to you, I'm sure. I'll say all that's proper and civil. What, must you go? Can't you spare me even a few minutes more? No? Well, I'll walk with you to the gate. By the bye, I saw you the other day, though you did not see me."

"Indeed! May I ask where?"

"In Meridian Square. You were pottering about! Had I seen any one to mind my horse I'd have got down to ask what the deuce was possessing you to hold a house-to-house visitation in a neighbourhood like that. The whole population must have been at one-o'clock dinner, I think. At any rate there were mingled odours of fish, onions, bacon, and cabbage, and not one of the aborigines visible. You *are* in a hurry! Good-day. Look in as often as you can. *Good*-afternoon!" And the Baronet, as he shut the gate after Mr. Sudlow, slowly closed one eye with a waggish expression of such infinite, if silent amusement, that it really seemed a pity there was no one at hand with whom he could share the excellent joke evidently in progress.

"Sulk away, my friend," soliloquised the Baronet. "The more you sulk the better I shall be pleased. You've had two or three nasty falls this afternoon, or I'm much mistaken. Perhaps for the future Jack will think twice before he again feels quite so certain he is as good as his master."

"So your niece is not at home," suggested Mr. Sudlow to the banker the first time he was fortunate enough to meet that gentleman.

"Where is she, then?" asked Mr. Gayre.

"Gone out of town."

"O! Gone for how long?"

"I do know—not till she has finished the round of all her friends, as I understand."

Secretly Mr. Gayre reflected that Miss Peggy's absence would not prove of long duration if it depended on that contingency; but he only said,

"Well, you see, Sudlow, you and I are the only people left in town. Soon I shall be the last rose—for you doubtless mean to take your departure shortly."

"Yes, I think I shall get away for a while," agreed Mr. Sudlow. "I never remember so slow a season."

"Take comfort; it is over, at any rate."

"Which way are you going, Mr. Gayre?"

"If you had asked me two minutes ago I should have said to North Bank; but as my niece is not there the journey would be useless. Sir Geoffrey is sure to be out."

"*He* has not left town," said Mr. Sudlow, in an aggrieved tone.

"Now his daughter is gone you may be very sure he won't stop long behind. I understood him to say some time ago he was only staying on her account."

"I suppose," remarked Mr. Sudlow, rue-fully, "he has plenty of friends always ready to invite him."

"Possibly, probably; but I really have no information on the subject."

"I daresay now he'll be going to some great place in the country to shoot."

"He may; I do not know."

"If I could speak French well I'd go abroad," said Mr. Sudlow, a little inconse-quently; "but it is such a nuisance to be in a foreign country, and experience a diffi-culty about even asking for a glass of water."

"If Sir Geoffrey were here he would advise you to get over that difficulty by never asking for a glass of water;" with which easy observation Mr. Gayre managed to end the dialogue and betake himself to Wimpole Street, whence he despatched a note to his brother-in-law, asking, "What have you done with Margaret?"

During the course of the following day back came Sir Geoffrey's reply:

"DEAR GAYRE,—Don't you trouble your head about Peggy. She is out of town, staying with friends—that is what Peggy is doing; and she is going to remain out of town for the present. As for myself, now I have that anxiety off my mind, I intend running down to Snatchwell's place in Staffordshire to have a turn among the longtails. You had better come too. Lots of game; pleasant house to stop at; colourless wife, with no harm or good about her; excellent cellar; host who likes his guests to enjoy themselves. Snatchwell would have been just the husband for Peggy—son of an ironmaster, or something of that sort, who left him a large fortune. But then, you see, there's Mrs. S.; and even for Peggy I don't feel disposed to bring myself to the gallows. If you like to look up any evening you name, shall be glad to see you;

but the place is all, after a manner, done
up in holland and brown paper, and there
are no servants except Sweet Lavender.

"Yours, G. C.

"Think about Staffordshire."

"Then she is really out of town," decided
Mr. Gayre. "I scarcely believed it. Who
can he have found to take charge of
her?"

CHAPTER IV.

LANDED.

SEPTEMBER had come and gone. Spite of Sir Geoffrey's gloomy prophecies concerning an early winter, that year summer, as if loth to part company with everything fair and beautiful, lingered in England till even in late November such a blue and sunshiny sky looked down on mead and stream and copse as often fails to gladden the eye in rose-laden and leafy June. It was October—a dry glorious October, with foliage turning red and yellow and brown and russet on the trees, when the cones hung low on the pines, and late pears and apples and plums shone mellow on the espaliers; and there was just enough of

chilliness in the autumn air to make a fire
pleasant, and the country looked its very
best, and the stubble gleamed golden in the
bright sunshine, and sportsmen winding
through woods only just beginning to get
somewhat bare and thin of foliage gave
animation to almost every sylvan landscape.

The Warren was looking enchanting.
Down in the plantations there was an au-
tumnal rustle and scent; but immediately
around the cottage it might still have been
July, so firm was the turf, so fair the
lawns, so bright the gardens, so gay the
verandah, with flower and leaf and berry;
whilst as for Mrs. Jubbins, the gladness of
Nature seemed reflected in her face.

So happy and good a season the widow
had never known. The glory of an Indian
summer was streaming across her life just
as the sunshine lay golden upon the Kentish
fields. Three, often four, days a week Mr.
Gayre now spent at her house.

Ostensibly he came to shoot; but then he might have found far more pheasants, far finer sport, elsewhere. Were not great houses open to him? Had not grand and notable persons asked for the pleasure of his company at their country seats? It was optional with him, she knew, whether he chose to chase "the wild deer and follow the roe" in Scotland, or kill a stray rabbit on his lordship's twenty-acre lot. For him the rivers of Ireland danced and glittered in vain, the Yorkshire moors held no charm, the stately hospitality of great men's houses presented no temptation.

At last, thought the widow, after the years, the long patient years, of waiting, he had become quite one of the family; and by Christmas perhaps—who could tell?— the day might be settled when, the last drop of bitterness extracted from her cup, she should exchange the name of Jubbins for that of Gayre. As regarded the banker

himself, she felt he had grown too delightful; while still superior to all created
beings, he was yet more human, more acces-
sible, less cynical. He took the keenest
interest in Ida's equestrian exercises; he
talked to the boys about their future—he
was very earnest that one at least of them
should pursue the path Mr. Jubbins had
trod before.

When he spoke about "oil" it seemed
to the widow that product became nectar.
Attar of roses never smelt sweeter than
rank sperm or olive when purified by Mr.
Gayre's clever tongue.

At last he was identifying his interests
with hers—"taking notice" of her children,
advising her—not coldly, but as one who
took a pleasure in the subject, as to their
future; and all this had come to pass since
she left Brunswick Square and migrated to
Chislehurst.

Blessed Chislehurst! blessed Warren!

thrice-blessed Lady Merioneth! As she paced the rooms once trodden by that noble personage, as her feet pressed the carpets formerly honoured by the foot-steps of nobility, and looked out of the windows on the woods for which her money paid, but in which Mr. Gayre shot, the widow forgot to remember she had been Higgs and was Jubbins—forgot everything in heaven and on earth save that she believed at length her long fealty was to be rewarded, and that ere long she would be solemnly asked whether she Eliza would take this man Nicholas for better and for worse.

Poor Mrs. Jubbins! Men were deceitful ever; and Mr. Gayre only made the few pheasants and rabbits he ever " potted " at The Warren an excuse for hearing tidings of Susan Drummond.

Since the great party they had met thrice—twice at Chislehurst, once at Enfield, whither Mr. Gayre repaired with a message (which might just as well have been sent on a post-card) from Sir Geoffrey.

It struck him Mrs. Arbery was not particularly delighted with his visit, and that Susan seemed a little anxious and *distraite*; but when next she walked with him round and about The Warren he could see no difference in her, save that she had grown more sweet and beautiful than of yore. When would Sir Geoffrey and his daughter return to London? That was the only question Mr. Gayre now accounted to be of any real importance. Politics were to him as vanity, and the state of the money market a matter of supreme indifference. He could not propose to Susan at The Warren, where his most telling sentence might be spoilt by a shout from one of Mrs. Jubbins' untrained and ill-mannered cubs. It was equally impossible to say what he wanted

to say out at Enfield, under the eye of
Mrs. Arbery. No; he had decided the
when and the where his declaration should
take place, if Heaven only so ordained
matters that his brother-in-law and niece
returned to North Bank before all sunshine departed. He knew the very spot
in the Regent's Park where he meant to
lay all he had of value on earth at her
dear feet. He would entice her there, and
before those wonderful brown eyes lay his
heart bare.

He had thought the whole affair out;
there was nothing to conceal, nothing of
which he need be ashamed. It was for
her sake only he had sought out his
relations, for whom he was now prepared
to do a great deal. Her will should be
his law. Aught a man may do he was
ready to essay, if only she would lay her
hand in his and say, "We will walk
through life together."

Occasionally perhaps he felt a twinge or two concerning Mrs. Jubbins; but if a woman likes to deceive herself, is a man to blame?

Mr. Gayre felt Miss Drummond was not likely to censure him greatly for not asking the widow in marriage. Susan moved among the City people; but she was not of them. She had scarcely a thought in common with the bulk of the persons Mrs. Jubbins knew. She was good to Ida, tolerant towards the boys; but O! and O! what a gulf, wide and long and deep, worn by centuries of culture and thought and breeding, lay between her and the rich dowagers who " condescended " to exchange a few words with Mrs. Jubbins' young friend, as she flitted about the place, getting a book for one, a few flowers for another, a cushion for a third —" making yourself cheap," so Miss Chelston once truly and indignantly remarked

—a thing, by the way, Miss Chelston was never likely to do.

As for Mr. Sudlow, he was wandering to and fro upon the earth, like a perturbed spirit. He had gone to every usual and unusual seaside resort within a reasonable distance of London, and nowhere found Miss Chelston, either in the flesh or in the visitors' list. She had vanished, and nobody apparently, except her father, knew whither; Mr. Gayre did not, or Lavender, or Mrs. Lavender, or the housemaid, or Mrs. Jubbins, or Miss Drummond. Mr. Sudlow had tried them all, openly and craftily; but it is impossible to tell what one does not know, and the suitor could only, by dint of trouble and time and scheming, extract at the last the answer he had received at the first.

"Miss Chelston was out of town with some friends." Nobody could tell when she would return, nobody seemed to know

whether she would ever return; nobody
was able to throw the smallest light on
Sir Geoffrey's plans for the future, save
that there seemed some idea of giving up
Mr. Moreby's box at Christmas.

"And I did hear a word let drop, sir,"
said Mrs. Lavender, smoothing down her
apron, "that very likely Miss Chelston
might winter abroad with a relation of
Sir Geoffrey's," which revelation was in
acknowledgment of a sovereign pressed
into the worthy woman's hand. Had she
vouchsafed this information at first instead of at last, she would never have
received that twenty shillings sterling coin
of the realm.

"Dem!" said Mr. Sudlow, as he flung
himself away, leaving poor Mrs. Lavender
utterly amazed. "Dem!"

Clearly if Sir Geoffrey failed to understand many good things, he had a perfect comprehension of such a nature as

that possessed by the son-in-law he hoped
to secure.

"Dem!" said that worthy, which mono-
syllabic curse meant he felt he must now
take action.

"And he went out of that there gate,"
said Mrs. Lavender to her spouse, "and
tore down the road as if he were a dog
with a tin kettle tied to his tail!"

A week later, Mr. Gayre had but just
finished dinner, and was in the act of
filling himself a glass of claret, when the
door opened, and, unexpected and unan-
nounced, Sir Geoffrey Chelston made his
appearance.

"I know you don't care to see me in
your house," began the Baronet, directly
the first greetings were over; "I must be
a confounded deal less sharp than I am
if I failed to know that. But under the
circumstances I thought you would not
mind. *Sudlow has proposed.*"

" No ! " exclaimed Mr. Gayre.

" Fact, my dear boy, and a deuce of a
time he has been about it, in my opinion.
If I had not packed Peggy bag and
baggage out of town, we should never
have got him up to the point. Yes, five
days ago I was staying with a young
fellow in Norfolk, who has just come
into fifteen thousand a year and some
splendid shooting—gracious Heavens, only
to think of the luck everyone seems to
have but myself!—when a letter arrived,
forwarded on from my club. It was
from our friend, asking my permission,
wanting to pay his addresses, and all the
rest of the business; a very proper sort
of epistle altogether, except that, apparently, he had forgotten all about money
matters; at any rate, he said nothing on
the subject. So I wrote back from Antler
Castle a diplomatic little letter, thanking
him for the honour he did my daughter

and myself; but intimating it was not exactly the alliance I desired. I didn't say what I wanted, but I made him feel he was scarcely in the rank—you understand."

Mr. Gayre did. The charming Baronet had pursued precisely the same tactics in his own case he was now practising on behalf of his daughter; but it was not necessary to go into that question, so the banker only said,

" Did he write again? "

" No, *he came.* By the greatest piece of good fortune, Dashdale—that's my friend, you know—happened to be at the station with tandem, dog-cart, livery servants, and everything likely to impress an out-and-out cad like Sudlow, when he heard that individual inquiring how he could get to Antler Castle. 'Who is it you want there?' asks Dashdale (a deuced ready off-hand sort of fellow Dashdale). 'Sir

Geoffrey Chelston,' says Sudlow. 'You're
not a dun, I hope!' cries Dashdale between fun and earnest. Sudlow, I believe,
got very red, and said, 'No, he wasn't a
dun.' 'Jump up, then,' says Dashdale;
'give him his head; stand clear, there.'
And before Sudlow was well settled in his
seat, as sweet a pair of bays as ever you
clapped eyes on were spanking along the
road at a pace which took away our
friend's breath.

"'If you believe me,' says Dashdale, 'the
cockney held on—held on, by—— !' "

"Well?" asked Mr. Gayre.

"Dashdale—most deuced hospitable man
—made him stop for dinner, stop the
night, stop for breakfast, stop for luncheon,
and then ordered round the brougham and
sent him over to the station. 'Any friend
of my friend Chelston,' said Dashdale, 'is
welcome to anything I can do for him.'
If I had coached him up, Dashdale could

not have played into my hands better. Of
course, in a house like that, Sudlow got
a glimpse of the usages of decent society.
Thank God, I am no snob. I would just
as soon eat a crust of bread-and-cheese at
a wayside pub as dine off silver; still, I
confess I was glad that, for once, Sudlow
should see the sort of thing I had been
accustomed to. There was not much
bounce left in him when he asked me for
half an hour's conversation in the library."

"And the end of it all?" inquired Sir
Geoffrey's patient auditor.

"I'm coming to that. He wanted my
daughter; what was my objection to him?
I said, 'General rather than particular. I
looked for something beyond mere wealth
in a husband;' and I fooled him into
believing Dashdale might suit me for a
son-in-law, as, indeed, he would, only he's
engaged to his cousin, a girl with the
wickedest pair of eyes, and the sauciest

smile, and the best seat across country you'd desire to see."

"Yes," said Mr. Gayre.

No revelation the Baronet could make would have surprised his relative!

"That arrow stuck. 'You see,' I said, 'you are *only* rich.' 'Surely it is something to *be* rich!' he urged. Of course I agreed to that. 'But then a great deal more is needed. In our rank we look for other things besides money. I am a great advocate,' I went on, 'for people marrying in their own set. My daughter would be miserable if asked to associate with persons beneath her.'"

"'I should not ask her to do anything of the sort,'" he declared.

"'I do not know,' I said. 'I have noticed a tendency in you to think people great and grand merely because they have so many thousands a year. In your estimation, if I may say so without offence a lord mayor is an individual to be culti-vated. Personally—though I am not in the least prejudiced—I would rather not associate with lord mayors, and I certainly don't intend to let my daughter associate with them. You have forced me to speak plainly,' I finished; 'and now no offence being, I hope, given, take my advice, and look out for some City heiress.' And with that I rose to end the conversation."

"It would have ended with me at a much earlier period," said Mr. Gayre. "How you can be so intolerably rude, Chelston, passes my understanding."

"Rude! I was particularly polite. I didn't 'Confound his impudence!' or bluster about my family. I was obliged to show him where he had gone wrong, but I tried to spare his feelings as much as possible. However, he would not let me go. He was willing to do everything in his power. A golden key would unlock

the door into almost any society nowadays;
and, with his money and my daughter's
beauty, birth, and breeding, he thought—
he felt sure, indeed—there would be no
difficulty in getting into the very first
circles."

"'Make no mistake about that,' I said.
'Society is not a theatre, where you have
only to pay your money and walk into
the stalls. Besides, what earthly reason
have you to suppose my daughter would
marry you? Has she shown the slightest
partiality for you?'"

"'Well, he could not say she had. Still,
he thought he might have a chance if I
would only give him opportunity;' and I
let him talk on and on, and at last over-
persuade me into giving a sort of reluctant
and conditional consent to his writing to
Peggy. He wanted to see her, but I
would not allow that. 'I can't have the
girl harassed as you have harassed me,'

I told him. 'She is a timid sort of creature, and it hurts her, I know, to give pain so much, she would be just as likely as not to say 'Yes' when she wanted to say 'No.'"

"Then he entreated me not to prejudice her against him. 'Honour bright,' I promised; 'if I say nothing in your favour, I'll say nothing in your disfavour;' and he was going to end with that, when I remarked, 'O, by-the-bye, before we go any further we had better understand each other about one thing—*settlements*.'"

Mr. Gayre smiled cynically, but Sir Geoffrey did not choose to see that smile.

"Would you believe," he said, "the beggar did not want to make any settlements; so we had a very stiff ten minutes before I could make the least impression on him. 'He did not approve of settlements.' 'Very well, then,' I said, 'you don't propose to my daughter.' 'Whatever the amount of her fortune might be, he would settle a similar sum.' 'Then,' I said, 'you don't propose to my daughter.' 'He would settle three hundred a year.' 'O no,' I said, 'you don't propose to my daughter. Hang it, sir!' I went on, 'have you come here to insult me? You've nothing *but* money to throw into the scale; and, by Heaven, if you don't throw in a good lot of that, wife of yours daughter of mine shall never be! Do you think I am going to have my only child left to the tender mercies of any husband? No, no, Mr. Sudlow, you have deceived yourself. I am not as simple as I look. I have not lived fifty years in this wicked world for nothing. And if my daughter marries, she shall marry as befits her station. Settlements liberal and all in order —good establishment—plenty of servants— carriage—everything in the best style— money no object whatever. Now you

know my views, and there is an end of
the matter.'"

"And Mr. Sudlow——?"

"Your friend accepted the inevitable.
'Pon my soul, there are people who like
you the better for thrashing them. When
I found out my gentleman's game I did
not spare him, and now he is as tract-
able as you please. He has my permission
to write to Peggy through me, and I have
told her she is not to take him at first,
but that she must take him at last. I
wish they could have been married immediately, but that's impossible. He has
to find a house *she* likes, buy furniture
she selects, purchase the carriage *she* prefers,
(if he behaves himself I'll give them a
pair of horses such as you don't often
see), make settlements to be approved by
my solicitors. Gad! when you think of it,
Gayre, marriage is an awful thing for a
man. Then, on the other hand, Peggy

must provide a *trousseau*—not a mere make-shift sort of business, but the best money can buy; and afterwards comes the worst difficulty of all—what are we to do with the girl in the period between the time she is engaged and married? There is only one person I can think of fit to matronise her. I must see Susan Drummond on the subject. She can help me in that quarter, I know."

"Do you think of going over to Enfield, then?" asked Mr. Gayre.

"To Enfield! Not I, faith! I am not so fond of cold water, old women, and sour looks as all that comes to. I'll just drop Susan a line, and ask her to run over and see me as soon as ever she can. We must take time by the forelock now, or else time may reverse the operation."

"But you don't suppose Miss Drummond will run over, as you call it, to see you?"

" Won't she ? Ah, you don't bet ; if you did, I'd lay long odds Susan will come at any inconvenience to herself. You don't know Susan—that's flat, my lad. And now I must go, and you will be very glad to see my back. It's a queer world, too. Only to think of the Chelstons and the Gayres, and the Chelstons and the Sudlows ! " Having delivered himself of which suggested parable, Sir Geoffrey, after stigmatising claret as cold unhealthy stuff, which thinned the blood and destroyed the digestion, poured himself out a tumbler of Mr. Gayre's rare vintage, and swallowing it with a wry face, as though it were medicine, walked out of the house with a gravity of demeanour and steadiness of gait which deceived Mr. Gayre's servant into believing the Baronet was soberer than any judge.

For one rash moment Mr. Gayre had felt tempted to declare Miss Drummond should not be at his brother-in-law's beck and call, that it was monstrous to ask the girl to come to North Bank even for ten minutes during his niece's absence; but the next, caution won the day; only he resolved that upon the very first opportunity which offered he would try to gain a right to stop all that sort of thing.

But then, good Heavens! if Susan married him she would be almost Sir Geoffrey's sister-in-law; and this seemed so utterly monstrous an idea that Mr. Gayre had, spite of his own will, to sit down and consider the complication of relationship which would ensue.

Aunt to Marguerite and Mr. Sudlow and the Minor Canonesses, sister-in-law to the Canoness and Canon Gayre! The banker felt quite disheartened.

"There ought to be some law passed to relieve people of these liabilities," he considered; and then he decided to haunt

North Bank till he heard when Susan might
be expected to pay that extraordinary visit
suggested quite as a matter of course by
Sir Geoffrey, if indeed she ever paid it at
all.

CHAPTER V.

BETWEEN WIND AND WATER.

" I ASKED you to come over in a way our worthy friend here evidently considers extremely free and easy, that I I might get ten minutes' uninterrupted chat with you. We've known each other too long to stand on ceremony, eh, Susan?"

"I should think so indeed," answered Miss Drummond, but the colour rushed into her face as she spoke.

"What on earth," wondered Mr. Gayre, "can make the girl blush so painfully at times, while on other occasions she does not seem to have a drop of tell-tale blood in her body?"

"Can you tell me where Miss Matthews is to be found?"

"She is living at Shepherd's Bush," answered Susan.

"There, I felt sure you could help me out of the wood. How is she off?"

"Not very well, I fear," was the reply.

"All the better for my purpose," said the Baronet gaily. "Sorry, of course, on her account, and all that," he went on; "but if she is not overburdened with this world's goods, she may be the more inclined to let bygones be bygones."

Susan shook her head gravely. "What is it you want her to do?" she asked.

"Come here for three months, and I'll make it worth her while."

"I am afraid," said Miss Drummond, pursing up her pretty mouth till it was like nothing so much as a sweet pink rosebud; then meeting Sir Geoffrey's eye, her lips opened, and she broke into a sudden and irresistible peal of laughter, in which the Baronet himself joined heartily.

"Faith, it seemed no joking matter at the time, Sue," he said, as soon as he could speak; "and there's Gayre wondering what the deuce we are laughing at."

"I can guess," remarked Mr. Gayre, with a poor semblance of merriment.

The three were at luncheon together. Mrs. Lavender had what she called "tossed up" a very pretty repast, over which Sir Geoffrey Chelston, clothed, shaved, and as sober as his previous night's doings would permit, presided. That luncheon was indeed his breakfast, and with the aid of several highly-seasoned and savoury dishes, assisted by strong cordials, he was trying to get that troublesome stomach of his into good temper.

"Have a glass of sherry, Susan, do," entreated the Baronet. "Capital sherry this.

Now I want you to coax Miss Matthews to come and take charge of the house for three months. I am sure she would do anything for you."

"I do not think she would do that," answered Susan, with an attempt at gravity creditable under the circumstances.

"Not if I promised to be a good boy and behave myself? She need not fear any recurrence of the indiscretion. Deuce take the girl! what's she laughing at now?"

"O Mr. Gayre," panted out Susan, "if you could only see Miss Matthews!"

"He need not wish to see her, I'm sure. Touch of the tar-brush about her complexion, and figure indescribable. But fact is, Gayre, I did offend Miss Matthews—as conscientious a woman as ever entered the house. An excellent person, but most confoundedly ugly—perhaps that was the reason she was good. There is no merit in ugly people being virtuous. I can't think what

the deuce possessed me; or rather—I know,
it was some of the worst whisky that ever
came out of a cheating innkeeper's cellar.
She needn't have made such a fuss about
the matter, though.　If she looked in her
glass she must have been perfectly sure
what I did was committed in a moment of
mental aberration.　Never previously," finished the Baronet, "in the course of a long
and, I may add, comparatively sinless life,
did I so far forget myself."

"She would not have minded it so much,
I am sure," interposed Susan, "if Dottrell
had not chanced unfortunately to come into
the room."

"Where, if you believe me, Gayre, on
my sacred word of honour, I was making
that worthy lady tread a measure like Young
Lochinvar.　I must have been confoundedly
drunk; not with the quantity, only with
the quality, of what I had taken.　And
when I got home and found the old girl in

the drawing-room, I believe I chucked her under the chin, and insisted she should dance a minuet with me. She declared I kissed her, too; and I daresay I did, for I was quite off my head. As a matter of choice, I wouldn't have done such a thing in my sober senses for a thousand pounds; and then, in the middle of the performance, Dottrell, our then butler, appeared on the scene.

"She appealed to him for protection, and straightway opened out on me. I sat down for the simple reason that I could not stand, and she did hold forth. Father Mathew and Mrs. Grundy together could not have hatched up such a discourse. She would have gone on till now, only Dottrell calmly remarking, 'You had better come away, ma'am; Sir Geoffrey does not understand a word you're saying;' with firm decision took hold of her arm and marched her out of the room."

"And the next morning?" questioned Mr. Gayre, who now began to understand more thoroughly than ever the reason why Sir Geoffrey found his domestic affairs somewhat difficult to manage.

"The next morning Dottrell woke me out of a sound sleep in order to deliver a letter from Miss Matthews.

"'Put it down,' I growled, for I had such a headache I could scarcely open my eyes.

"'Beg pardon, Sir Geoffrey, but Miss Matthews wants to catch the 11.25 train, and——'

"'Let her catch her train, and be blanked to her!' I said, settling down again, for I had clean forgotten all about that last night's minuet. But it was of no use. Dottrell proved too much for me, and I had to sit up and face the matter.

"'Won't she take an apology?' I asked.

"No, she wouldn't; all she meant to take was her salary and departure. But now, look here, Susan. You tell her I'm a reformed character; and that I'm never at home till morning: and that you'll go bail for my good conduct; and that Peggy who is now quite grown up, and a dragon of propriety, keeps me on my best manners; and that she shall have fifty pounds for the three months, paid in advance. She'll come then, bless you! she'll come. If she should want any further guarantee, refer her to Gayre. He'll tell her the man never lived who had a greater respect for elderly women than myself. Why, rather than offend one of them, I'd keep out of their way for ever."

It was too much. Even Mr. Gayre had to laugh, as if he saw some fun in the Baronet's utterances, while Susan faithfully promised she would say all she could in Sir Geoffrey Chelston's favour.

"And you'll say it this afternoon, won't you?" he entreated, "because time happens to mean money to me just now."

To this arrangement Susan at first demurred a little. The afternoon would be far advanced before she could get to Shepherd's Bush. Miss Matthews might not be at home. Mrs. Arbery would certainly feel uneasy. But each of these points Sir Geoffrey combated, and she yielded; the while Mr. Gayre sat inwardly fuming at the way his brother-in-law made use of the girl, and the manner she allowed herself to be so treated. Mr. Gayre failed to see the beauty of making oneself cheap. He could not understand that the moment Susan began to think she was of too much importance to answer to the beck and call of those she cared for, she would cease to be Susan Drummond, and become a totally different person.

"If you are going by the Metropolitan,"

said the Baronet, by way of conclusion, " we can walk together as far as Baker Street. Will you come with us, Gayre?"

Almost gnashing his teeth, Mr. Gayre said he would. Where was now his chance of speaking to Susan? He felt at his wits' end. He did not know what to do. Should he write? Should he go down to Enfield, or wait his opportunity, or——

" This is your hat, Gayre," cried Sir Geoffrey, interrupting his meditations, " and here is Susan. I always did say I never saw a girl who could put on her bonnet as fast as you. However, as you know, a ' bonny bride is soon buskit;' which reminds me that I am to be father, and give you away some day. You remember our compact?"

" Very well indeed; and I will hold you to your promise," answered Susan.

And then, as Mr. Gayre held the door open for her to pass out, he wondered to himself what on earth his ladye-love could see in such a reprobate as Sir Geoffrey to laugh and make merry with him and smile on his battered wicked face, as though it were pure as that of an angel.

Nevertheless, they were a pleasant trio as they walked to Baker Street; and Mr. Gayre, after he had got Susan's ticket and seen her into the train, he and Sir Geoffrey accompanying the lady on to the platform per favour — lamented his own want of daring in failing to take a ticket also to Shepherd's Bush.

But if there is a 'divinity which doth hedge a king,' there is a higher divinity which hedges a modest, innocent woman. Not for all the world would Mr. Gayre then have so timed his proposal as to hurt the girl's self-respect, and daunt her fearless self-reliance.

"She has no business to be running about London in this way by herself," he thought;

but he felt he dared not be the man to teach Susan Drummond she was doing wrong.

Next morning's post brought a note to North Bank saying Miss Matthews utterly declined to accept Sir Geoffrey's offer; but she—Susan, the writer—had met, at the house of Margaret's ex-governess, a lady willing to enter upon the duties he required at once.

" I am sure she is just the person you would like," finished the fair scribe; " *not young* " ("Good Lord!" groaned Sir Geoffrey), " a widow " ("'Ware hawks, but she can't catch me," considered the juvenile Baronet); " rather nice-looking and pleasant-mannered" ("That's a bit of comfort"); " has a grandson she wants to keep at school " ("Then she must be out of her teens, at any rate "); " and seems to be in all respects the sort of person you require. I enclose her address."

To which Sir Geoffrey replied:

" You settle with her, my dear Susan. Anything you say I'll stick to. If she can come into residence before the week is out, so much the better."

Upon which authority, it may be assumed, Miss Drummond acted forthwith, since Mr. Gayre was duly and truly informed " an elderly party was coming to keep things straight at North Bank."

" She'll be a deuce of a nuisance, I know," finished the Baronet; " but we must have something of the sort. Those few days I had to stay at home and play propriety after the Chislehurst spread nearly killed me. Besides, my time is my money; and it wouldn't pay me to play the part of Mrs. Propriety. Once Peggy has given a sort of modified consent, she shall come home; and I've asked Susan to tear herself away from the delights of Enfield, and stay with us for a while to brighten up the house."

It was not long ere Mr. Sudlow won a

reluctant and dignified acceptance from Miss Chelston.

"She feels she scarcely knows enough of me yet," explained Mr. Sudlow to Mr. Gayre; "but even that looks well, does it not?" asked the happy lover, invading the sanctity of Upper Wimpole Street one morning before Mr. Gayre had finished his breakfast. "She would not have said so much if she had not intended taking me some time, would she?"

Declining to commit himself to any positive statement, Mr. Gayre nevertheless admitted he thought his niece must, at all events, be entertaining the idea of Mr. Sudlow as a husband.

"I am afraid Sir Geoffrey will be very hard to deal with on the subject of settlements," ventured Mr. Sudlow.

"Time enough for you to consider that question when you have arranged matters with my niece."

"You know I object to settlements——"

"So I remember you said before; and we need not go over that old ground again. Keep your objections for Sir Geoffrey. It is his daughter, not mine, you hope to marry."

What Mr. Sudlow wanted to know was whether Mr. Gayre meant to behave handsomely on the occasion. Five thousand pounds, he hinted to Sir Geoffrey, would not empty the Lombard Street coffers, while it might prove of material assistance in the housekeeping battle; but the Baronet warned him off this treacherous ground.

"Gayre is a deuced odd sort of fellow," he said; "and if he is going to give anything, he'll give it without being asked— perhaps slip a *dot* into his niece's hand when she is going away to change her dress. But a certain person, who shall be nameless, couldn't get sixpence out of him

unless he took the notion. Our best plan
is to let him alone."

Which was all very well for the Baronet,
considered Mr. Sudlow; but not so well for
the person undertaking to board, lodge, and
dress the beautiful Marguerite for the re-
mainder of her days.

"You see it is not as if Miss Chelston
had a fortune in her own right," ventured
Mr. Sudlow at last.

Mr. Gayre looked at him and smiled.

"I suspect," said the banker, "if Miss
Chelston had possessed a fortune in her
own right, or in right of anybody else, Sir
Geoffrey would not have bestowed it on
you. Take my advice—if you get youth
and beauty, and birth and breeding, don't
break your heart because there is not
money too. You could not have got one
of the four in the person of my niece but
for the folly of Sir Geoffrey Chelston, formerly of Chelston Pleasaunce."

"You seem to consider my wealth nothing."

"On the contrary, it is your wealth which has given you the chance of marrying my niece; and when you are married to her I hope you will live in a manner befitting her rank and her means. And for Heaven's sake, Sudlow," added Mr. Gayre, with sudden energy, "give up collecting your own rents. Dunning weekly tenants is scarcely an employment suitable for a man whose wife may one day hope to be presented at Court."

Mr. Sudlow turned pink and scarlet, and blue and crimson, in about as many seconds; and his moustache quivered as he asked,

"Who told you I did anything of the kind?"

"Sir Geoffrey. He says he saw you doing it. And now do take a word of advice. Your social future is before you to make or to mar, and, what is of a great deal

more importance to me, my niece's future
can be made or marred by you. If you
mean to continue to do these sort of things
say so, and the matter shall be broken off
at once. It is quite competent for you to
lower yourself; but my niece shall not be
pulled down to your level. Why, in
Heaven's name, don't you sell all that
wretched property, and try to put your
many talents out to interest in some way
befitting a gentleman?"

"Whenever you can prove your ability
to introduce me to really good society," retorted Mr. Sudlow, "I will follow your advice. Meantime permit me to say I do not
consider the persons I find you know most
intimately are in any respect superior to
myself."

"You had better repeat that statement
to Sir Geoffrey Chelston," said Mr. Gayre,
"and ascertain his opinions on the subject.
I was wrong to interfere in the matter. It

does not much signify to me whom his daughter marries, or whether she ever marries at all."

With which explicit statement Mr. Gayre rose, and would have ended the conference, but that Mr. Sudlow, with profuse apologies, begged him to overlook his little ebullition of temper.

"You *are* hard on a fellow, you know," he finished. "You delight in catching me up and twitting me for taking care of my money; though you would be the first to find fault if I squandered what my father left me."

"But for my grandfather your father would not have had much to leave," answered Mr. Gayre.

And then the talk drifted away from the dangerous question of rank to the surer ground of money, and peace seemed restored by the time Mr. Gayre announced his intention of starting for the City; and

Mr. Sudlow asked him to come round by Bond Street, as he wished to buy a ring, and desired the benefit of his experience.

"I do not profess to be any judge of jewelry," answered Mr. Gayre; "but I will accompany you with pleasure, though I consider your purchase somewhat premature. However, if the ring is never possessed by my niece, it will do for some other young lady; only there is the loss of interest to consider, Sudlow."

"I don't care a straw about that," declared Mr. Sudlow, valiantly. "Once your niece says 'yes,' and if only those confounded settlements can be arranged, I shall be the happiest man in England."

"That's what they all say before marriage," commented Mr. Gayre, searching about for his umbrella.

They were just turning into Vere Street as a cab pulled up opposite Marshall & Snelgrove's. Before the driver could get

down, a small gloved hand turned the
handle, and in a second the owner of that
hand was on the pavement, and helping
another lady to descend more slowly.

" Why, it is Miss Drummond! " exclaimed
Mr. Sudlow; then he stopped; for the flash
of glad surprise in Mr. Gayre's face, and
the eager step made involuntarily forward,
were revelations more extraordinary than
welcome. A man could scarcely have
clapped hands during the fraction of time
it required to make the banker's secret
plain reading to Mr. Sudlow; and then
both gentlemen were raising their hats and
greeting Susan, and remarking how extremely strange it was they should have
met.

The cabman duly paid and discharged,
Miss Drummond introduced the banker and
his companion to Miss Matthews, during
the progress of which ceremony it tried
even Mr. Gayre's gravity to look upon the

highly respectable lady with whom, in the
great drawing-room at Chelston Pleasaunce,
his brother-in-law had essayed . to trip a
measure. Nearly six feet tall, gaunt, short-
petticoated, with slim ankles and lean legs,
and long, thin, flat feet, with a face like a
horse, kindly dark eyes, black hair turning
gray, a good Roman nose, prominent teeth,
more than a suspicion of a moustache : a
less likely woman to appreciate the delicate
attention of being chucked under her chin
never existed.

As for Susan, she felt she dared not
look at Mr. Gayre ; there was a sus-
picious twitching about her mouth and
a tremor in her voice Mr. Sudlow could
not comprehend, though both phenomena
were perfectly intelligible to his companion.

"Going shopping, Miss Drummond ?"
asked Mr. Sudlow, who, in his new character of an almost engaged man, had al-

ready commenced to take an interest in so purely feminine a weakness.

" Yes, really," answered Susan, with a little nod and a happy smile, and that sudden and vivid blush which was beginning sorely to perplex Mr. Gayre. What on earth could make her colour up at such a simple question?

" I always envy ladies their ability to sew and their liking for turning over silks and satins," observed the banker.

" My purchases," said Susan, " must be of a much more modest description; " while Miss Matthews didactically observed, she did not know what ladies would do without the resource of needlework.

As there probably never existed anyone less able to suggest even a vague solution to such a conundrum than Sir Geoffrey's brother-in-law, wide though the field of speculation opened up by Miss Matthews' sententious remark might be considered,

the banker wisely declined to enter on it.
Instead he inquired when Miss Drummond
meant to go to North Bank, and finding
" Very shortly—next week, perhaps," took
his leave, and, accompanied by Mr. Sudlow,
walked off, followed by warm encomiums
from Miss Matthews, who professed great
astonishment that her former employer
could be possessed of so desirable a relative.

" And what is the younger gentleman's
name, Susan ? I failed to catch it."

" Mr. Sudlow—a captive of Margaret's
spear and bow."

" Will it come to anything ? "

" I don't know. I hope not. He is only
rich."

" If he is rich, then you ought to wish
it may come to a great deal. Margaret
would be wretched married to a poor man;
and she must be far happier and safer in
the house of a husband than residing

under the roof of her reckless and dissolute father."

"Poor Sir Geoffrey!" remonstrated Susan. "You are far too hard upon him."

"No, indeed, my dear, I am not; and the only fault I have to find with you is that you wilfully shut your eyes to the real character of that dreadful man. I am so sorry you are going there; it is really not respectable for a young girl to associate with a person who bears so bad a character as Sir Geoffrey Chelston."

"He has never been bad to me," retorted Miss Drummond, sharply — "always good and kind and thoughtful. One can only speak of people as one finds them."

"Ah, Susan——"

"Now it is of no use, Miss Matthews," interrupted the girl, with that decision which often astonished Mr. Gayre; "I shall always like Sir Geoffrey. I should like him even if he picked pockets."

"So he does," said the Roman Con-
queror, as the Baronet had been wont to
call his daughter's governess; "so he does,
if all accounts be true."

"I don't care whether they are true or
false. What is the use of being fond of a
friend only when he does right? I should
want my friends to be fond of me if I
did wrong—as you would be, you know
you would; so never ask me again to turn
my back on Sir Geoffrey."

As days went by, the object of all this
charming loyalty might have been regarded
almost as a reformed character. The
Baronet was devoting himself to getting
his daughter well settled with the same
earnestness he brought to bear on betting,
card-playing, and horse-dealing.

"Sudlow finds those settlements a rasping fence," he said to Mr. Gayre; "but he
shall take it, by——! or give up all hope
of Peggy;" and because he was stead-

fastly purposed to frustrate the slightest
attempt to balk the jump, he rose be-
times, and stayed about the house, and
watched over Miss Chelston, who was
now at home, like a hen with one
chicken. The engagement at length became a fact accomplished, and Sir Geoffrey
was pleased to signify that he would
put no obstacle in the way of a speedy
marriage.

"You satisfy my lawyers," was his terse
way of putting the case in a nutshell to
Mr. Sudlow, "and you'll satisfy me. To
save all trouble and argument, I have given
them their instructions, by *which they will
abide;*" and if any disinterested person had
been by to see the shake of the head with
which the Baronet emphasised this utterance, he could not have imagined that Miss
Chelston's worthy papa was destitute of
worldly wisdom.

For, indeed, there had come a certain

change over Mr. Sudlow which puzzled and annoyed Sir Geoffrey. It was not that he cared for his lady-love less; but he certainly seemed in no hurry to endow her with the amount of his worldly goods upon which the Baronet insisted. That meeting with Susan Drummond told him how small the fair Marguerite's chance of inheriting her uncle's wealth might be considered, and hitherto he had always calculated that she would, sooner or later, come in for a good slice out of Lombard Street.

He longed to tell Sir Geoffrey and his daughter what he had discovered, he was waiting his opportunity to do so; but he did not wish to show his new card before Mrs. Morris, who sat constantly on guard doing lace-work, which she sold to various patronesses for the benefit of her grandson, whose school-bills were made the excuse for that sort of genteel begging greatly in favour with ladies so situated that they are obliged to wrest a living from society by hook or by crook.

He earnestly desired to get the matter off his mind before Miss Drummond again appeared at North Bank, and at length his chance came one evening, when Mrs. Morris had been obliged to go to bed with a severe headache, and Sir Geoffrey was fidgeting about the room, trying all the easy-chairs in succession, and thinking what an awful nuisance a daughter was, and wondering why Lady Chelston could not, excepting for contrariness, have presented him with a son instead, and marvelling when Mr. Sudlow would take his departure, and feeling sure there had never existed on the earth before so exemplary a father as himself.

Something was said about Mr. Gayre not coming so often as formerly to North Bank.

"I suppose," added the Baronet, "the

fact is he has other fish to fry at Chislehurst. I confess I feel rather surprised
at his choice myself. I hoped he might
have gone in for something different; but
money attracts money, there can be no
question about that."

"And Mrs. Jubbins is so immensely rich,"
put in Miss Chelston, softly.

"Are you quite sure it is Mrs. Jubbins,"
asked Mr. Sudlow.

"Why, of course, man," answered Sir
Geoffrey; "who else is there? Who else
should there be?"

"I daresay you know best," said Mr.
Sudlow; "still, I have a notion that when
Mr. Gayre marries it will not be the
wealthy widow."

"You speak as if you had some one in
your eye," exclaimed the Baronet, roused
into attention.

"So I have."

"And who is she? O, pray tell us!"

entreated Miss Marguerite. "What I would give to see her!"

"You can compass your desire without any great expenditure of either time or money," said Mr. Sudlow, triumphantly, for he felt the moment for making a *coup* had come. "Unless I am greatly mistaken, Miss Drummond will be metamorphosed into Mrs. Gayre before we are any of us much older."

"Susan Drummond!" repeated the Baronet, sitting bolt upright in his chair, and holding the arms with both hands, while Margaret, literally, for the moment, bereft of speech, remained dumb. "I think you are wrong there, my friend," added Sir Geoffrey, after a pause, which seemed to last for years.

"Am I?"

"How in the world could such a notion have got into your head?"

"I can't imagine how it failed to get

into yours," answered Mr. Sudlow, with a fine scorn.

"Poor dear Susan, what a preposterous idea!" said Miss Chelston, gently.

"You will find it a true one, I imagine," persisted the new prophet.

"Fancy Susan my aunt!" suggested the beauteous Marguerite, in the sweetest accents, the time her heart was full of rage and malice and all uncharitableness.

"You might get a worse, Peggy, but never a better," said the Baronet, who, having now grasped the position, decided there was something in it. "If the land lies as you think, Sudlow, I for one shall be delighted. On the face of God's earth there walks no grander woman than Susan Drummond; and while I should have made the Jubbins welcome, I'd go out of my senses with delight if matters turned out as you think."

"You are very disinterested, Sir Geoffrey."

" Not I, faith ; I know Susan would never take from my girl for herself. She'd be the making of Gayre—and—and—us all. I wonder how it was I never thought of such a thing? Gad, if it had rested with me they should have been man and wife long enough ago."

Mr. Sudlow opened his mouth to reply, but an imploring look from Miss Chelston caused him to shut it again. "After all," she said, "my uncle may not have an idea of the kind."

"I hope and trust he has," cried Sir Geoffrey. "You have brought me the best piece of news to-night, Sudlow, I have heard for this many a day! Susan married to Gayre! why it sounds too good to be true. I'll go straight away down to him, and ask if there's anything in it. We can walk part of the way together;" and the Baronet rose from his chair with all the more alacrity that he thought he now saw his way to getting out of the house and rid of his future son-in-law at the same moment.

"For heaven's sake, Sir Geoffrey, do no such thing!" entreated Mr. Sudlow. "Your brother-in-law would never forgive me if he thought I had been meddling in his concerns. Whatever you do, pray keep my name out of the affair; or, rather, refrain from mentioning the matter at all. I—I may be mistaken; but I considered it only right to give you a hint. I did not know the match was one you would like. I fancied there might be objections, both on the score of age and fortune."

"Did you?" said Sir Geoffrey, grimly. "Understand, if you please, I consider Susan Drummond a fortune in herself. Why, with her family and Gayre's money, they might do just what they pleased: and as for that trifle of disparity, Gayre is a good fellow, and deserves a good wife:

and, faith, if he gets Susan, he'll have something to be proud of."

"I never admired Miss Drummond particularly myself," remarked Mr. Sudlow—for which diplomatic speech he was rewarded by an appreciative glance from his ladye-love—"but from the first hour he saw her I know Mr. Gayre did."

"Showed his taste," commented the Baronet. "However, I'll take no notice of what you have told us. Never spoil sport has always been my maxim. Upon my soul, I feel as much pleased as if anybody had given me a thousand pounds."

Which creditable feeling was certainly not shared by his charming daughter. She knew exactly what Mr. Sudlow was thinking, and her own opinion chanced to be identical with his. If Mr. Gayre married Susan he would not feel disposed to endow his niece with all he possessed. Miss Chelston had long fastened her gaze on the Lombard Street

coffers, and it could not be said she regarded with pleasure the idea of Susan
getting any share of the spoil.

"Don't say anything more about this
before papa," she hinted, during a brief
absence of Sir Geoffrey for the purpose of
draining a bumper to the health of the
future Mrs. Gayre. "Do you think my
uncle is really thinking of marrying dear
Susan?"

"I am quite sure he would like to marry
her," answered Mr. Sudlow; and then he
explained how the knowledge had come
upon him like a flash of lightning. "'Pon
my honour, a child might have knocked me
down," he finished.

"It was wonderfully clever of you," said
Miss Chelston, with a pleasant flattery of
voice, and word, and look; "but then you
are so clever. Don't you think the disparity
is dreadful, however?"

"Yes; but if Miss Drummond does not

mind that, I am sure Mr. Gayre need not."

"O, don't; I can't bear to think of it," murmured Miss Chelston, shuddering; and then Sir Geoffrey, refreshed and invigorated, sauntered back into the room, where he began to yawn with such good effect that Mr. Sudlow felt reluctantly compelled to say good-night.

"Now, look here, my girl," said Sir Geoffrey to his daughter, as he took his hat, preparatory to getting the "cobwebs blown off him," "take my advice, and neither mell nor meddle in this business. You'd love dearly, I know, to stop the match, but it will be a deuced fine thing for you should it ever come off. As for Susan, if she can fancy your uncle—and he is not an old man for his age; he hasn't had to bear the anxiety I have—I'm sure she'll never repent taking him. When she comes here keep a quiet tongue about the matter. We'll want your uncle's help yet,

I'm afraid, in that matter of the Sudlow fish; so for the Lord's sake don't let any of your woman's whimsies put his back up."

Only to a certain extent did Miss Chelston comply with Sir Geoffrey's wishes. Miss Drummond spent a few hours at North Bank one day, and promised to return shortly and stop for a fortnight. It was then she and her friend had a serious talk about the Sudlow engagement.

"O Margaret! don't marry him; don't, like a darling," entreated Susan, at the close of a long and confidential interview. "You do not care for him, and you do care for Lal Hilderton."

Miss Chelston laughed scornfully.

"Should you recommend me to marry Lal and make as good a match as you seem disposed to do?"

"Perhaps not," said Susan, "for there is that reason, you know, which might cause anyone to feel afraid of marrying Lal; but you have led him on and on, and—"

"Now, remember, I cannot bear being lectured, more particularly by you," interposed Miss Chelston.

"Well, then, tell Mr. Sudlow you can't marry him, and I won't say another word. Recollect, so long as I have a home you need never want one. And I am sure—"

"Make yourself very sure, dear, I mean to marry Mr. Sudlow. I shall not so far insult my own taste as to say he is the man I would have chosen. But beggars, you know—"

"O Maggie, Maggie!"

"O Susan! At the end of twelve months I wonder which of us will be the best off?"

"Good-bye, then, you poor mistaken child, and remember what I said."

"I certainly shall not forget a word you have said, dear;" and with a sweet smile,

Miss Chelston kissed her friend and saw Susan depart, and then sat down biding her time, which arrived that evening before dinner.

Mr. Sudlow was in evidence; Sir Geoffrey in high spirits, because his brother-in-law had walked up to North Bank; Mrs. Morris was putting the finishing touches to her toilette; Mr. Gayre was looking at the evening paper, when, in quite an artless and gushing manner, Miss Chelston opened her first parallel.

"I have such a piece of news for you, papa," she said, gaily.

"Good news, Peg?"

"Very good; it concerns Susan Drummond."

"Let's hear it, then," cried the Baronet.

"She is going to be married"—involuntarily Sir Geoffrey turned towards Mr. Gayre, but that gentleman never moved nor stirred, neither did the crisp sheet he

32—2

held rustle—" to Oliver Dane. You remember Oliver, don't you? Old Mr. Dane's grandson," went on the fair Margaret, almost without a pause, and maintaining an admirable composure. " He is at present in some house in the City—Colvend and Surlees—but he is going to start on his own account, whatever that means, and the wedding is to take place before Christmas."

" I don't think it will," said Mr. Gayre from behind his newspaper ; and as he spoke a dead silence fell on those present—they were waiting to hear more.

" *Mr. Oliver Dane,*" proceeded the banker, deliberately folding up the *Globe,* " *was this day charged at the Mansion House by his employers, Colvend and Surlees, with forgery and embezzlement, and remanded, bail being refused.*"

CHAPTER VI.

THE BLACKNESS OF NIGHT.

EARLY next morning Mr. Gayre was making his way into the Camden Road. Overnight, pacing the silent desolate streets, he had decided what to do. He would break the news to Susan. Unless Fortune meant to turn utterly against him, he felt that he should be the first to carry the tidings out to Enfield, and so score one trick in a game that would require the most careful playing. While his niece was firing her shot about Oliver Dane, it had seemed to him that he fell from heaven to earth. The whole time occupied by her narrative could have been reckoned by seconds, yet years ere then had appeared to him a shorter period.

How he had held his paper so that it did not even rustle, how he compelled his voice to utter the words he spoke without a tremor, were mysteries he could not have explained himself. Save for a certain ring of triumph in his tone he was unable to repress, Oliver Dane and Susan Drummond might have been total strangers to the banker.

This was the hidden rock he had always instinctively known stood in his way to port. Now he fully understood the reason of Susan's unaccountable blushes. At last he comprehended why she was at once so friendly and so indifferent. Everything which had puzzled him about the girl was clear at last; far, far too clear. But she could not marry this man. All was not lost. On the contrary, in this awful trouble he would be of such comfort, he would so watch over her, so sympathise with her every mood, that for very gratitude's sake she must at length give him love. And then he strove to think he would rather not change matters even if he could. It was far, far better she should have had a lover and found him worthless. At his age it was scarcely to be expected a young girl could give him the first, romantic, unreal dream-love of a woman's life; but the love that lasts would be his—the love founded on a rock—on respect, esteem, reason, and affection. No more wild, unpractical, dangerous friendships with handsome young fellows like Lal Hilderton; no running about at the beck and call of that sinful reprobate Sir Geoffrey; no more gallops with her easy familiar cousin the centaur. The brightness of her morning was gone, and she would now settle down and make a more charming wife, with the traces of tears on her cheeks, than she ever could have done in the sunshine of a ridiculous and impossible engagement.

It is always wise to make the best of a

bad bargain; and as Mr. Gayre rode leisurely along, he became so exceeding wise that he finally felt thankful such a person as Oliver Dane was in existence.

"I will make myself necessary now," he decided; "and, when her sorrow is a little spent, she will not be able to do without me."

A pleasant vision, truly. Poor dear Susan, with those wonderful brown eyes, coming to him, not as a ministering angel, but as a sorely wounded dove, weeping out her grief on his bosom, sobbing her tears in his arms, feeling him a tower of refuge in her time of trouble, and giving this disinterested suitor the last, best, strongest love of a strong unselfish nature!

Men of Mr. Gayre's type are all too apt to imagine Providence delights to play into their hands.

Certainly on that autumn morning, between six and seven o'clock, Mr. Gayre felt God was on his side.

The longer he thought about the matter the more satisfied he became that things were working round to promote his own happiness and Susan's welfare.

Out of evil good would come. When she had got over the fret of losing her lover, she would bring him, Nicholas, the whole of her great, loyal heart. Had the man died, had untoward circumstances separated her from Oliver Dane, she might never have recovered the blow. But forgery, embezzlement, the dock, and a felon's doom, must, he argued, hurt a woman's pride, and crush her love, and clear the course for a suitor like himself, unexceptionable in all respects save that unlucky item of age. Not for one moment did it ever occur to Mr. Gayre that Oliver Dane might be innocent. He knew Colvend and Surlees well. Mr. Colvend, indeed, kept his private account at Gayres', and he had often heard that gentleman speak in almost affectionate terms of young Dane, "remanded on the previous afternoon, bail being refused."

He was aware that at one time Mr. Colvend had thought of taking his clerk into partnership. Such a termination of the business connection was spoken about both by Mr. Colvend and Mr. Surlees. Of late Mr. Surlees, however, had seemed dissatisfied with their *employé.* The question possessed so little interest for Mr. Gayre, that when both principals wrangled a little about Dane, he only considered that person a bore; but now he remembered all their utterances, and came to the conclusion the young man must have been engaged in a course of fraud for years. He knew Mr. Dane's appearance perfectly well —his voice, accent, and manner had always struck the banker as quite unsuitable to his actual station.

" A gentleman to the backbone, sir," old

Mr. Colvend remarked; and now that "gentleman" was as good as convicted.

"Surlees is not a person to show mercy," considered Mr. Gayre. "It will be penal servitude. Well, not so long ago he would have been hanged!" Cheered by which consolatory reflection the banker proceeded on his way.

It was a lovely morning. The Seven Sisters' Road looked its best as Mr. Gayre rode along. Tottenham Valley, which lies just behind the Manor House Tavern, seemed literally steeped in sunshine; the morning air blew fresh and pleasant; the ground was hard, and echoed cheerily the sound of the horses' hoofs. Yes, though the blow had been severe, Mr. Gayre felt he was recovering from it. Things were not so bad that they might not have been a great deal worse. This trouble, properly utilised, must draw Susan nearer to him —nearer and nearer still. Now he knew his ground, and he had never known it before. Putting up his horse at a tavern in Enfield Highway, he walked on to Mrs. Arbery's house. As he pushed open the small gate he caught the flutter of a woman's dress in the garden; and, next moment, Susan turned and saw him.

"Why, Mr. Gayre," she cried, "what has brought you here so early? How is Maggie? There is nothing wrong with Sir Geoffrey, is there?"

She did not know, she had not a notion of the trouble impending; and for a moment Mr. Gayre's heart smote him when he thought of the sorrow he was bringing to the dear fair girl, who had never looked sweeter or lovelier than at that instant.

"My niece is well, thank you," he answered, "and Sir Geoffrey was well also when I saw him last night. I have come to see you, Miss Drummond. I want to tell you something I think you would rather hear from me than—strangers."

" Something bad?"

" I feel you will—I know you must— think so."

" Whom does it concern?"

" Mr. Dane."

" My God!"—her lips rather shaped the words than said them—"is he ill, *or dead?*"

" Neither. But let us go into the house. This garden is so exposed, and—"

Without a word she led him into the pleasant drawing-room, which commanded a view of Sewardstone and the Essex hills; shut the door close; and then, turning to the banker, said,

" Now, what is it?"

" I bring very bad news." He hesitated.

" I know you do; what is it, Mr. Gayre? Don't keep me in suspense. What is it you have come to tell me?"

"Have you read this morning's paper?"

"No, I have not looked at it. Oh, Mr. Gayre, what is wrong—what has happened?"

For answer he produced a copy of the *Times*, which he had bought on the road, and gave it into her hands, indicating a particular paragraph.

"I thought," he repeated, "you would rather hear of this from me than another."

She did not answer. She was reading the brief passage in yesterday's police report, which told her her ship had gone to pieces on the breakers. She finished it to the end; then lifted her eyes to Mr. Gayre's with a look of dumb entreaty which haunts him even now.

"My love! my love!" she murmured, and sat down transformed.

The Susan of old would never walk among the flowers in Mr. Arbery's garden again. That Susan was dead and buried

and Mr. Gayre stood marvelling to see the
change. Coming events cast their shadows
before; and the banker now understood
that yearning look in those sweet brown
eyes. The minor chord that gave such
a strange sadness every now and then to
the music of her young life meant that
trouble was on its way to meet her—the
crushing trouble she now saw face to face.

Minutes passed, but she never spoke.
After that one cry of agonised despair
she sat silent and motionless, while Mr.
Gayre, unable to suggest one word of
comfort, stood looking at her, with a
great pity and a wild jealousy and a mad
joy all contending together in his breast.

Through the window which looked out
on the Essex hills, bright sunshine fell
in golden bars across her hair, her white
soft throat, her hands lying loosely clasped
together in her lap. The girl's whole
attitude was that of utter abandonment.

For the moment she seemed stricken down.
She and hope and youth and gaiety had
shaken hands and parted. To have seen
her then, any one might have imagined
Susan Drummond would never laugh or
smile or jest again. The iron had entered
into her soul. *Forgery, embezzlement!* The
words were branded on her heart. The
man she knew so well, the man she loved,
accused of such awful crimes! It appeared impossible; and yet there before
her eyes lay the story in black and white.
His accusers said he had forged their signature; the proceeds of his imputed crime
were found at his lodgings. The notes
paid over the counter of the Union Bank
were discovered in his portmanteau, which
was packed as if for a journey. What
did it all mean? Tossing in a sea of
distressed conjecture, Susan still held fast
to one saving rope—*he was innocent.* If
the whole world declared him guilty she

would not believe the verdict. In some moment of mental aberration she might have committed a great sin (Susan felt she would do wickedness for the sake of those she loved); but Oliver Dane? No! While the sun rose and the sun set she could never believe that. He might have faults, and he had—Susan knew them— but he was perfectly incapable of such an act as this. He would want her. Vaguely this blessed thought began to shoot up— two fair green leaves of promise to beautify the arid desolation of the barren land to which she had been so suddenly transported. He could not do without her help. He had no relation, she knew, who would come forward at such a crisis. To all useful intents and purposes, he and she stood utterly alone in the world. Adam and Eve were perhaps less solitary in the Garden of Eden than her lover and herself in what some persons consider this over-populated world.

Directly that idea of help crossed her mind, she looked at her watch, and said,

"There is an up-train in about twenty minutes. I shall just be able to catch it, Mr. Gayre, if you will excuse me."

"Catch it! Where are you thinking of going?"

"To Oliver. I must go to him at once, you know——"

"No; by Heaven, that you sha'n't!" broke out Mr. Gayre, fiercely; then recollecting himself, he added, "Can't you trust me, Miss Drummond? Only say what you want done, and I will try to do it. If time, or money, or influence can help you in this strait, command all so far as they are within the compass of my power."

"Thank you," she answered, earnestly, "thank you;" and almost involuntarily she stretched out her hand, which he took and held in both of his while she went on. "We are so lonely, Mr. Gayre; we are so far more lonely than any human being could imagine."

He bent his head and kissed her hand —that white hand which she made no attempt to withdraw, which lay in his as a frightened bird nestles in the palm of someone who has rescued it from fear and death.

"If you can trust me —" he was beginning, when the door opened and Mrs. Arbery's voice was heard exclaiming a little sharply:

"What are you doing? Breakfast is ready, Susan." Then, catching sight of Mr. Gayre, who was standing very close to her niece—indeed, quite bending over that young person in a manner which seemed to indicate private communications of importance were passing between them

—she added, in a tone of severe and astonished dignity, "I *beg* your pardon, I am sure."

"Come in, aunt," said Susan, "we are not talking about any matter which can be kept secret. Will you tell her, Mr. Gayre?" and the girl turned her face, from which all the delicate rosebud pink had flown, towards the window, and looked with unseeing eyes at the distant hills, while the story of Oliver Dane's downfall was recited for Mrs. Arbery's benefit. It was a long story which did not take long in the telling. The bare facts contained enough of sorrow and disgrace without any necessity for further detail. Mr. Gayre said as little as he well could, but that little proved more than sufficient. If Susan's lover had been tried, convicted, and sent to penal servitude, Mrs. Arbery could not have felt more fully convinced of his guilt.

She listened to the narrative in utter silence, and when it was finished said calmly,

"I am not at all surprised."

"No?" questioned Mr. Gayre, for Susan did not speak.

"He is a young man I never liked," Mrs. Arbery explained. "It was an engagement I never approved."

"You cannot mean, aunt, that you believe him guilty?"

"I certainly do not mean that I believe him innocent. Everything is against him."

"Yes," said Susan, bitterly. "Everything is against him, everything has been against him; but that is no reason why you should think him a thief. Do you suppose if I heard you or Will had committed any sin I should believe the story? Oh, aunt, though you dislike Oliver, do not be hard on him. I can't

bear to hear you speak against the man
I am going to marry—I can't, I can't!"
and her voice trailed away into low
sobbing.

Mr. Gayre looked at Mrs. Arbery, who,
laying her hand on Susan's shoulder,
said,

"My dear, I do not wish to be hard
on him. If he has done wrong he is
suffering for it; but as for your ever
marrying him now, of course—"

"Are we not to have any breakfast
to-day?" cried Will Arbery at this point
in his mother's diatribe. "Why, what
has happened? What is the matter?"
he went on, looking in astonishment at
the group collected at the upper end of
that long pleasant drawing-room. "What
is wrong, Susan?"

"Don't tell him," pleaded the girl; "let
him read it;" and as Mr. Gayre handed
the *Times* to the young man in silence

she rose, and, twining her arm about her cousin's neck, looked over his shoulder while he glanced at the brief report.

"O Susan, I *am* sorry for you!" he exclaimed. "What ought we to do? Mr. Gayre, you know, I suppose, how we can be best of use."

"You believe him innocent, Will?"

"Innocent! Of course I do. It is some awful mistake; it can be nothing but a mistake," he added, turning to the banker.

From the manner in which he uttered the words they might have been intended either as an interrogation or a statement of opinion. Mr. Gayre chose to accept them in the former sense, and gravely answered that he hoped so.

"Mr. Dane may be able to explain the circumstances. As yet, you must remember we have only heard one side—that of his employers. When his statement is made the whole complexion of the affair will probably be altered."

"I do not need to wait for his statement," said Susan, with streaming eyes. "I know."

Mr. Arbery took a few turns up and down the room.

"Don't you think," he asked, appealing once again to Mr. Gayre, "the thing for me to do would be to see Mr. Colvend at once?"

"Better let me do so. I know both the partners."

"It—wasn't at your bank, was it?" hesitated Mr. Arbery.

"No; the Union. Mr. Colvend only kept his private account with us."

"What sort of a man is he?"

"Extremely kind. At one time he took the liveliest interest in Mr. Dane's future."

"Do you know Oliver, then?" asked Susan, drawing a quick gasping breath.

" I have seen and spoken to Mr. Dane.
Had I been aware you were interested in
him, Miss Drummond, I should have made
a point of cultivating his acquaintance."

"Standing here talking," remarked Mr.
Arbery, in a general sort of way, "won't
mend matters. Mother, if you will give
me a cup of tea, the sooner I get off the
better. Cheer up, Susan; I'll bring you
back good news, never fear."

" I am going with you," she said.

" No, Susan," said Mrs. Arbery. " Understand that I distinctly forbid your doing
anything of the kind. I will not have you
compromise yourself. You know what I
have been impressing upon you for a very
long time past. You thought me prejudiced,
and now you see something far worse than
ever I imagined has come to pass."

" It is quite true," answered Susan—
" something much worse than any one
could ever have imagined has come to

pass;" and she sat down again with something more nearly approaching a sullen expression clouding her face than Mr. Gayre had ever seen disfigure its fair beauty before.

"Shall I send *you* a cup of tea, dear?" asked her aunt, apparently quite unconscious of having given any offence; "it will do you good." But Susan only shook her head.

"Come into the other room, or Mr. Gayre won't touch a morsel; and he has ridden a long way to do you a kindness," whispered Will Arbery. Whereupon Susan rose, and, taking her cousin's arm, walked silently across the hall.

Mr. Gayre watched her at the morning meal, which was the great meal of the day in Mrs. Arbery's house.

She allowed herself to be helped to ham. She accepted a proffered egg. She took a piece of toast. She did not again decline that cup of tea, suggested as though a cup of tea were a panacea for all the ills of life. She made pretence of cutting up and toying with her food; but she touched none of it. She never looked at nor spoke to any one. She asked no question. She made no remark. Will Arbery argued out the Dane complication exhaustively, and Mr. Gayre exhibited considerable ingenuity in suggesting plausible reasons why it seemed the most natural thing in the world for three hundred pounds, paid over the counter at the Union Bank, on the strength of Messrs. Colvend and Surlees' forged signature, to be found in the lodgings of one of their clerks, a trusted *employé*, a gentleman they had once thought of taking into partnership—but Susan made no sign.

Mr. Gayre then shifted his ground. He spoke of the high opinion he had always entertained of Mr. Dane, of the conviction he felt from the beginning he was far too clever to be hampered with two such partners as Colvend and Surlees.

"Excellent men," proceeded the banker, warming to his subject, "but fifty years at least behind the times. Colvend's notions are those of the last century."

Just for the moment a faint flush, or quiver of the eyelids, or pitiful tremor of the mouth rewarded these utterances; but it was uphill work, and Mr. Gayre felt he was growing almost as anxious for the moment of departure as Mr. Arbery professed himself to be, when suddenly Miss Drummond's eyes, which she had lifted for a moment, became larger and brighter; her whole manner changed; her colour came and went, and, exclaiming almost incredulously, "It's Sir Geoffrey! it really is Sir Geoffrey!" she ran out of the room and opened the hall-door, and met him in the middle of the straight prim gravelled walk.

"Why, Susan, my girl!"

"O Sir Geoffrey!" and then the Baronet found himself, for the first, and, it may be added, the last, time in his life, holding in his arms a perfectly respectable young woman utterly beside herself with grief and anxiety, and what she considered a lack of intelligent sympathy.

"There, then," said Sir Geoffrey, stroking and soothing her down exactly as he might have done had she been a horse, "take it quietly, my beauty. There's nothing really to be frightened about. Dane—Dane's all right, you know. Gayre and I will stand bail for him. Tut-tut! what's all this trouble? Bless the creature, how she clings to me! There's nothing wrong; there is nothing to trouble you! You are safe now your old papa Geoff has come to the rescue. Bless you, he'll go and rout up the magistrates, and make them send your lover back to you at once. It is an outrageous proceeding. Never heard of such a thing—never in all my life. Now, now, now, don't cry any more. If you do, you'll not be able to see him when he comes back. What's that you are saying? I don't think him guilty, do I? You silly little mortal! Why, I'd just as soon believe myself capable of doing such a thing ; " which comparison struck Susan even in her then state of mind as scarcely conveying the amount of comfort Sir Geoffrey amiably intended.

"Dry your eyes, Susie, and come into the house and tell me all you know about the matter, and we'll see what's best to be done."

With which and such like fatherly words of rebuke and encouragement Sir Geoffrey led Susan into the drawing-room, where, as he stated, to his immense astonishment, he found Gayre.

"God bless me!" he exclaimed, "to think of meeting you, of all men in the world, here! Why, I'd ten minds to call for you on my way—I passed the end of your street. I've never been home all night—but I made sure you were snugly tucked up, dreaming of Consols and Lord knows what besides! Now, I call this really friendly of you. I was just saying, Mrs. Arbery," he went on, as that lady, frigidly decorous and deeply exercised in her mind, made her appearance on the scene, "that among us we'll put things right for our little girl."

"You mean very kindly, I am sure," answered Mrs. Arbery, "but there are some things which never can be put right. If you could only persuade my poor Susan of this, you would be performing an act of the truest friendship."

"We'll see about all that after a while," answered the Baronet cheerfully; "time enough to discuss all those sorts of questions when Dane is able to put his oar in. Now, Susie, wake up and say what you want me to do. As I told you, I haven't been to bed at all, but that makes no difference— I am ready to go anywhere and see any one."

"I want you to take me to see Oliver," murmured Susan, in so low a tone her words failed to reach Mrs. Arbery's ear.

The girl was still holding Sir Geoffrey's arm, and almost whispered her request. Just for a moment the Baronet looked grave, then he said briskly,

"So I will—so I will. Run and put your bonnet on, and we can talk as we go up."

"Sir Geoffrey," broke in Mrs. Arbery, "I really cannot allow my niece to go to London with you."

" Very sorry indeed to hear it."

" Her engagement has been a source of disappointment, trouble, and anxiety to me ever since I first knew of it."

" I can well understand that. Engagements very seldom do meet the approval of any save the pair engaged, and their satisfaction seldom lasts beyond a week after marriage. I myself think the whole thing a mistake ; but, bless your soul, you might as well try to prevent the sap rising as hinder two young people falling in love."

" Young people should fall in love suitably."

" So they ought," agreed the Baronet ; " but then, you see, as a rule, they don't, and in this world we have to deal with things not as they should be, but as they are."

" That is very true, Sir Geoffrey," answered Mrs. Arbery, who in her own family and amongst her own friends conducted herself after the fashion of a Mede and Persian; "and it is precisely because I object to things as they are that I feel bound to forbid my niece to hold any further communication whatsoever with Oliver Dane."

While Mrs. Arbery was speaking, Sir Geoffrey felt Susan's hand slip from his arm, and saw her gliding out of the room through the nearest door. He listened gravely to all the "elderly party" had to advance, then took up his parable.

"In my best days," he began, "I never was what is called a ladies' man" (Mr. Gayre smiled grimly); "but I believe I understand the sex; or, to be more exact, I feel the sex is made up of a number of women differing mightily from each other, which is a fact your ladies' man never can grasp. I don't attempt to generalise men. Why should I attempt to generalise women? And so, to return to what I had to say, don't you curb up Susan too tight. If you do she'll give you a lot of trouble. Take the right way with her, and, bless your soul, I'd undertake to drive her with silken thread; take the wrong way, and—"

"So far as I understand your mode of speech," said Mrs. Arbery, white almost with passion, "you mean to encourage my unfortunate niece in pursuing a line of conduct opposed at once to propriety and common sense?"

"I always lament having to disagree with a lady," said Sir Geoffrey, with a low bow—the one gentlemanlike talent the Baronet possessed was his bow, afoot or on horseback—"but as you drive me into a corner, I feel bound to tell you plainly I consider propriety and common sense were never opposed to anything Susan Drummond liked to do. If you can show me that they were, I will abandon common sense, and 'go in' for another and better sense called Susan Drummond."

"Bravo, Chelston!" cried Mr. Gayre, almost involuntarily. In acknowledgment of which the Baronet said:

"All right, Gayre; thank ye."

"And despite of what I say, and Mr. Gayre said when he first came this morning, you actually mean to take Susan to see a felon?" went on Mrs. Arbery.

"Softly, softly," entreated Sir Geoffrey. "Wait at least till the man is proved guilty before you call him hard names. And even supposing the worst comes to the worst——"

"Which it must," interrupted Mrs. Arbery, with great decision.

"Well, even in that case, I don't think it would be well to use such a word when speaking of Oliver Dane. We are none of us infallible. We don't know what we might do if we were tempted. A man may make a mistake, but—"

"These fine distinctions are quite thrown away on me," retorted Mrs. Arbery. " Right is right, and wrong is wrong."

" Oliver has done no wrong, aunt," said Susan, re-entering the room at this juncture. " Give me some good wish before I go—some good wish for both of us; " and she held up her sweet face to be kissed.

But Mrs. Arbery would not kiss her. Once again she expressed her disapproval of the whole expedition, and was especially irate against her son, who, declaring Susan should go where she liked, and that he would go with her, drew his cousin's hand within his arm, and angrily left the house, leaving Sir Geoffrey and Mr. Gayre to follow at their leisure.

CHAPTER VII.

SIR GEOFFREY'S IDEA.

IT was a fortnight later. Oliver Dane
had once again been brought before
the magistrate, and committed for trial.
The evidence against him was conclusive;
not a creature except Susan believed in
his innocence. Even Sir Geoffrey, who
said he was "deuced sorry for the fellow,
deuced sorry indeed," shook his head
mournfully, and lamented over the weakness of poor human nature which, he
implied, was alone responsible for ruining
the whole, future of "as promising a young
man as you would wish to see."

"Heaven only knows," he exclaimed,
"what demon could have possessed him.

I am sure **any** of his friends would have found the **money.** I would, if I'd had it, and there were **lots,** I'll be bound, **in** the same mind. That **woman** getting the cheque cashed **was** a bad **sign**—a widow too—and handsome, ah!" and Sir Geoffrey shook his head. "There **must have been** some **screw** awfully loose. Wherever a woman leads, trouble follows. **Wonder** who she is? Awkward **mess** altogether. **Dane** is the last man in the **world** I should have thought likely to go **wrong** in that way; but, dear me, **what** a dance any petticoat may lead the **best** of us! You and I can't be too thankful, Gayre, can **we?**"

"Some persons are **more** lucky than wise," agreed **the** banker, thinking Sir Geoffrey **was** a **case** in point.

"That is very **true.** It is not always the best rider clears the ditch. But, as I was saying, **it is** altogether a most confoundedly **awkward business.** Though I am sorry for Dane, I don't think he is doing right, and I told him so. 'You ought to plead guilty, and settle Susan's mind,' I said. 'If the case were mine I could not keep a girl on the tenter-hooks. This sort of thing might be all very well in dealing with a man, but it isn't fair to a woman.'"

"And what did he say?" asked Mr. Gayre.

"Just the usual thing—that he could not tell an untruth even to settle Susan's mind; that he had not forged the signature; that the money was forwarded to his lodgings by some one unknown; that he had his suspicions; that unless he could change them into certainties it would be worse than useless to speak; that he quite understood it was impossible for Susan now to marry him; that the engagement must be considered at an end; that his life was wrecked; that she, the noblest of women, must not sacrifice her life through any mistaken idea of loyalty to him; that her devotion was the bitterest drop in a bitter cup; that he had not the slightest hope of an acquittal; but that he could not plead guilty, or tell Susan he was dishonoured in deed as well as in the eyes of the world. Then I said, 'Your boasted affection is a very poor sort of affection; I would not treat any girl after such a fashion. I am disappointed in you. I· knew your father to be a fool, and your grandfather a screw, but I did *not* think you were a scoundrel.'"

"Rather rough on the fellow," commented Mr. Gayre.

"Rough! not a bit too rough! 'Look at what the consequences will be!' I said. "'Susan is just the girl to exalt you into a sort of martyr. She will go on believing in and fretting about you. She will lose her youth and her good looks. She will not marry, and, if she do not die, she will live a sad sweet old maid, nursing other folks' babies instead of her own.'"

"You drew quite a touching picture," said Mr. Gayre.

"And *then* he wouldn't," declared the Baronet, with a great oath. "No, —— me if he would! I don't know when I went through such an interview, and without a drop of anything either to give me a fillip. Give you my word, Gayre, I felt quite exhausted when I came out. Had to go into the nearest pub, and ask leave to sit down. It's heartless, you know; that's what it is. Hang it! I'm not particular, you are aware. If a man commits a crime I wouldn't turn my back on him; but to keep on with this sort of infernal humbug to a girl like Susan Drummond, why—why, it's the very deuce!" finished the Baronet, who was delivering these sentiments in his own house and at his own table.

"I suppose it is not on the cards that the man may be, by possibility, innocent?"

" Innocent! for Heaven's sake, Gayre, don't you get sentimental! It's all very well to humour Susan's notion for a while, and let the girl down gently; but we, who have been out in the world, and know a thing or two, must not talk like children. Run your eye over the whole matter. Here's a young fellow brought up by a grandfather, who won't allow him sixpence of pocket-money, and puts him into an attorney's office. Young fellow won't be an attorney, goes and enlists; old Drummond buys him off, and has him stopping at the Hall for a while. Then he falls in love with Miss Susie; grandfather, delighted, thinks she will be an heiress; grandfather finds out she won't be an heiress, and insists on the engagement being broken off; young man comes up to London in a huff, and, through favour, get's into Colvend's house. Everybody believes it's all over between him and Susan. Eventually the grandfather makes some conditional sort of promise to find money enough to buy a small share in the business. After a while, Surlees begins to find fault with the young man, the idea of the partnership is abandoned, and Dane announces his intention of going into business on his own account. Grandfather discovers he and Susan mean to be married, and declares he will cut young man off with a shilling. Young man has got a little into debt, and wants money besides for capital. Surlees gets a hint that all is not square, and begins to look into matters, which present some serious complications. Holds his tongue to make quite sure—means to speak to Dane when he has all the proofs complete. At that juncture a three-hundred-pound cheque, signed Colvend and Surlees, is presented across the Union counter and paid. Notes are found in Dane's rooms, in a portmanteau ready packed. Make what you can of the case, my friend—it looks confoundedly black against Mr. Oliver."

" Yes," agreed Mr. Gayre—" yes."

" But there is no good in talking to Susan yet. I told you exactly what would happen if Mrs. Arbery persisted in taking up the curb another link. Most foolish, self-opinionated old woman. Thinks because she won't drink half a pint of ale, the Almighty has given her dominion over every living thing that moveth upon the earth. If she had only let Susan go her own way at her own pace for a while she would not have sent the girl mad, as she has done. When she told me about Susan having left Enfield, and taken up her abode with Miss Matthews, I said, ' It's your own fault, ma'am ; she'd never have got the bit between her teeth if you'd driven her easily. But, bless my soul and body, there are other persons in the world who have a will beside Mrs. Arbery. No—excuse me—

I can't get the girl back; and if I could, I wouldn't try. The end of it will be she'll marry Oliver Dane.'"

"But you don't really think that likely?" exclaimed Mr. Gayre.

"I'll tell you what I think—that Dane won't marry her. How could he? The dear grandfather will give him nothing; Susan has but two thousand pounds. Say he only gets a couple of years, what will he be fit for when he comes out? No, the thing is not to be thought of. But our plan at present is to take no notice—to her, at any rate. After the trial we'll see what we had better do."

"Miss Drummond appears to have no doubt of his innocence."

Sir Geoffrey shrugged his shoulders. "All the fault of the old party out at Enfield Highway. She would tighten that curb. It's just the same with a woman as a horse; and you know, Gayre, the result of fretting a young high-spirited creature by holding it in when there's no need to do anything of the sort. Bless you, I always try to give them their head for a bit; and if Mrs. Arbery had taken no notice, and let Susie have her own way about this confounded business, the girl would have begun to entertain doubts concerning her lover, and wanted to know who the woman was, and why Surlees could not get on with friend Oliver, and so finally come gradually round to a sensible view of the matter; whereas—" and the Baronet, finding words inadequate to express the pass to which Mrs. Arbery's management had brought affairs, poured himself a good measure of champagne into a large tumbler, "throwing on the top," as he expressed the matter, "just a flavour of brandy."

If Sir Geoffrey had not been a baronet the mode in which he tossed off this bumper and smacked his lips approvingly

after it might have been considered vulgar;
but circumstances alter cases, and circumstances altered most cases with Mr. Gayre's
brother-in-law.

"Ah," said Sir Geoffrey, leaning back
in his chair, stretching out his feet to the
fire, and looking with an air of childlike
contentment at the leaping flame, "you may
talk as you like about your clarets—!"

"I am not aware that I have spoken
about clarets at all," mildly remonstrated
the banker.

"Deeds speak as loud as words, and
you always drink that poor thin sour stuff
—for poor and thin and sour it is, though
you do pay a price which makes my hair
stand on end; but then a rich banker is
one quantity and a poor baronet another.
However, as I was remarking, you may
depend upon it a man's face takes the
cast of the tipple he affects. Now claret
produces lines, wrinkles, and gives a sneer-

ing sort of expression to the countenance. I'd drop it if I were you, and go in for something more generous and exhilarating. Why should you look older than your age? You are a mere boy in comparison to the battered craft you are good enough to call brother-in-law. Let me see, you are younger than poor Margaret— "

The banker shook his head.

" Well, the difference either way, I know, is very trifling, and we know what a baby thing she was when I married her. Why don't you turn your attention to matrimony, Gayre? If you can't make up your mind to the widow—and I suppose you can't or you'd have been step-father to the Jubbins fry long ere this— there are plenty of girls who, I am sure, would be only too glad if you could be induced to say a civil word to them."

" I fancy you are right about the widow," went on Sir Geoffrey, finding his brother-in-law did not speak. "Of course she has money; but then you have plenty of your own, and money is not everything, though it is a great deal, as nobody knows better than I do. Why shouldn't you marry, and have a nice wife and pleasant home? You're just the sort of fellow girls would take to, and make up romances concerning. I know them; bless your soul, they'd turn you into a hero, and fall down and worship at once. Think of it, Gayre. 'Pon my honour, I don't like to see you drinking claret and living in a big house all alone, with only servants about you. Providence never intended such a thing. It is you that have made the mistake; but you may remedy it yet."

"If I take to champagne and brandy and making love to young ladies?" questioned the banker.

"I don't suppose you would care to make love to old ladies, which, by-the-bye, reminds me of something I wanted to say to you. I shan't be able to induce Mrs. Morris to stop on; and I declare solemnly I have not chucked her under the chin or insisted on her dancing a *fandango*."

" Why does she wish to go, then ? "

" The usual thing; all women are alike; they have a craze for what they call respectability, and a knowledge of what constitutes impropriety, which knowledge I myself regard as sinful. Mrs. Morris has arrived at the conclusion this house is not an abode in which she ought to continue to reside. She has her doubts about it and me. She fails to understand why visitors do not call; why my daughter is not asked out; why we never give parties; why you have not Peg staying in Wimpole Street; why I can't be induced to return to six o'clock tea, nine o'clock prayers, and eleven o'clock bed; why we have not more servants; why we do not keep a

carriage; why I run household bills; why
I do not pay every fellow who has a
'heavy account to make up.' She feels,
in fact, the air of North Bank may be
injurious to her social health. It seems
she has got a presentation to Christ's
Hospital for the boy. So now, as she can
do without me, she means to leave. Nice
and grateful, is it not?"

"How extremely awkward!" said Mr.
Gayre.

"I wanted her to stop till Peggy was
married, but no she won't. 'My dear
Mrs. Morris,' I urged, 'you have surely
reached a time of life when you might
be able to defy Mrs. Grundy and all her
works.'"

"'No woman is ever so old as to be
able to disregard appearances, Sir Geoffrey,'
she replied; 'and for myself, though I
have a grandson—'"

"'Yes, yes, yes,' I interrupted, 'I know

you were married at sixteen and your daughter at fifteen—the usual thing—so you can't be much over thirty; but still—'"

"'Pardon me,' she returned, 'I am over forty (upon my soul, Gayre, she must be close on seventy), but I feel it is as imperative for me to regard my character now as I did when I was in my teens.'"

"'Most creditable, I am sure,' I replied; 'but forgive me if I ask what is the good of shouting "Wolf!" when there is not an animal of the sort outside the Zoological Gardens? Let us walk across and see the wolves, Mrs. Morris, and say you will stop a little while longer.'"

"But she wouldn't, Gayre; she was as stiff as you please. She set her lips tight and she drew down her nose (have you ever remarked the stiff-neckedness of Mrs. M.'s nose?), and looking straight at me,

and, fixing me with those steel-blue eyes
of hers, said, 'You must excuse me,
Sir Geoffrey, but my mind is quite made
up. Miss Matthews told me from the first
your place would not suit me, and she
was right. The place does not suit me;
and if I may venture to say so, your
place would not suit any gentlewoman who
respected herself.' "

"What are we to do about Maggie,
then?"

"That is just what I wanted to talk
over with you. I have been trying to get
one of Lal Hilderton's old aunts—people
I had Peg with when they were in Wales
—to come up from Richmond and take
charge, but it was no use. They say
she has treated Lal iniquitously, and that
in consequence their dear nephew has
taken to smoking, drinking, and going to
the deuce generally, which of course is
pleasant for a father to hear."

"My fair niece can't help flirting, and I do not think Mr. Lionel Hilderton required any goading along the road to ruin."

"Precisely my own idea; thank you, Gayre. Now I am going to propose something I know will astonish you, but don't make any rash comment till you have considered the matter in all its bearings. *The right person to take charge of Peg is her mother;* and if you'll help me a bit with the pecuniary part of the matter, I am willing to let bygones be bygones, and for the sake of my girl make it up with your sister."

"You cannot be serious, Chelston."

"I never was more serious in my life. I have a right to take back my wife if I like. The story is an old one now. At the time many persons thought Margaret was dead, many imagined we separated by mutual consent, many that I was the sinner; only a very few knew the rights of the case.

Well, we make it up, we take a small house somewhere, and there's your natural protector for Peg at once. Bless you, I've thought it all out, and feel sure this is the course we ought to pursue. Don't say anything yet. Mrs. Morris does not remove the light of her countenance for a month. Think it over: a mother for Peg, a home for Susan, who can't live always with that gruesome old maid at Shepherd's Bush, all trouble and anxiety ended, a very small additional allowance from you, and the thing is complete. I never was a man who thought of myself, and I assure you I have forgiven Margaret from the bottom of my heart over and over again. She was a very sweet girl, that sister of yours, Gayre, and I can see her now as I saw her that day we first met at Brighton;" and the Baronet stooped, as though to hide a tear, while his brother-in-law rose and paced the limits of Mr. Moreby's dining-room.

At last he said,

" You *have* indeed taken me by surprise, Chelston."

" Yes, I thought you would be astonished," said Sir Geoffrey, in the tone of a modest man who felt serenely conscious he had performed a good action.

" You say you do not expect me to give you an immediate answer."

" Take your time—take your own time," observed the Baronet, tolerantly. " I am the most considerate man on earth. No person can say with truth I ever made capital out of my matrimonial troubles. Now did I ? "

" I am very sure you never did," agreed Mr. Gayre, thinking as he spoke that he knew the reason why.

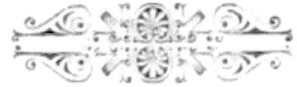

CHAPTER VIII.

THE TRIAL.

WHATEVER small amount of comfort it may be possible to extract from being the principal figure in a *cause célèbre* was denied to Oliver Dane. Nothing could have been more prosaic and commonplace than his trial. As usual, the Old Bailey was crowded; as usual, the benches were filled by that curious class of persons who are to be found in all parts of London—lounging on the seats of the Thames Embankment and Leicester Square, in the waiting-rooms of railway stations, and the Law Courts and the few other places of free resort—engaged in the herculean task of killing time. Before a comparatively unappreciative audience the great scene in his life's story was played out. Fashionable ladies were conspicuous by their absence. Stock Exchange gentlemen, with their hats well on the backs of their heads, and their hands deep in their trousers-pockets, utterly failed to put in an appearance. The thousand shades of business to be met within the confines of the City likewise felt the case was one which presented no attraction. A defaulting clerk, a common case of forgery and embezzlement : " Pooh ! not worth crossing the road to hear."

A good murder or a big swindle would have attracted an appreciative audience; but the crime of which Oliver Dane stood accused being common as picking pockets, it was before a comparative speaking empty house, Messrs. Colvend and Surlees' *ci-devant* clerk made his bow.

Through the windows of what is called the Old Court the gray lights of a winter's day streamed coldly upon audience, judge, aldermen, barristers, jury, and prisoner, who was young, rather over middle height, slight, well-formed, dark-haired, dark-eyed, standing looking calmly at the judge, and quiting himself, as even Mr. Gayre could not but acknowledge, like a man. Confinement and anxiety had worn, but not otherwise changed, him. He was still the Oliver of those happy blissful days which now seemed further away than childhood. And Susan, who, with a little bunch of forget-me-nots fastened prominently in her dress, had come to sit out the trial, when she saw the dear face of old in such a place, felt the hot tears coursing slowly down her cheeks and dropping heavily behind her veil. On entering the dock for one moment he glanced around, and in that moment she made the slightest gesture with her hand and touched the knot of blue flowers nestling in her breast. That was all—but he knew. And then, turning his gaze resolutely away, he never again let his eyes stray towards her—never once till the trial was over and the torture ended. Mr. Gayre sat on one side of the girl and Miss Matthews on the other. Will Arbery had left England, and all other friends were either witnesses for the defence or too angry or indifferent to support her lover at such a crisis. But for Susan, Oliver Dane might well, just then, have felt himself forgotten by God and forsaken by man. Innocent or guilty, it seemed as though his fellows had deserted him. In his cell he had not felt half so lonely as he did in the crowded court. Mr. Gayre he had seen and Miss Matthews likewise. Mr. Surlees stood near the dock leaning against a partition. Familiar as he was with the City, as a matter of course, the names and appearances of many men present were known to the prisoner. He recognised his solicitor talking to a man he concluded must be the counsel engaged for his defence ; a burly coarse-looking individual, famous for his still in brow-beating witnesses, he was aware had been retained for the prosecution. He saw the place of honour under the canopy filled by an ex-Lord Mayor, gorgeously attired, with the 'sword of justice' hung over his head on the wall behind his seat; then his glance wandered to the judge, and after that his thoughts began to stray.

It seemed as though all the sin and misery of the centuries rose out of their forgotten graves, and came trooping, ghostly phantoms, into the place which had witnessed one terrible scene of their earthly tragedy. The prison taint was around him, the prison smell in his nostrils. He could see the dock filled with wretched men and despairing women; widows' sons and gray-haired sires; fingers, soon to be cold and still in death, playing nervously with the herbs, placed to preserve those who were free from prison fever, fever kept for the benefit of the captives.

Old stories, long forgotten, recurred to memory; all the legends of that shameful place, where in the name of "Justice," so many innocent men were condemned in the good old days to infamy, torture, and death, came jostling his elbow, laid their skeleton hands on his throat, thrust their pallid faces between him and the judge, and glided—a ghastly, awful procession—down the stairs, from step to step of which they carried, in dumb agonised silence, the burden of their woe.

All at once a voice brought him back from dreamland to the fact that he was the latest member of that terrible crowd. On the boards where such tragedies had been enacted it was his turn to play a minor part.

"Guilty or Not Guilty?"

"Not Guilty, my lord."

And then Mr. Gayre knew Sir Geoffrey's pleadings had been, after all, in vain.

"It will be of no use urging extenuating circumstances after that," thought the banker, looking hard at the accused, while a feeling of pity, inconsistent in a merchant and a rival, stirred his heart.

At once the court settled to work. The prosecutor's case was fully stated. No detail which could hurt the prisoner and his friends was spared; his birth, education, antecedents, means, failings, were shouted in the ear of the public.

He was shown to have been always somewhat wild—a boy hard to control, impossible to train ; a lad determined to take his own course to perdition ; a youth destitute of gratitude, who turned and stung his best benefactor, an old and infirm gentleman of large fortune and the possessor of extensive estates.

" Our learned friend is a master of his craft," thought Mr. Gayre, himself not wholly indifferent to the suggested iniquity.

Sledge-hammer work the learned counsel evidently considered quite good enough for the Old Bailey and Oliver Dane ; and accordingly down he came, mercilessly crushing all flowers of grace and beauty the young man's life might have been supposed to hold. Everything charming, in word, deed, or manner, was either a sin or a snare—often indeed both. He had bowed his grandfather's gray hairs low with sorrow ; he had been seen on racecourses drinking champagne and betting freely ; he had utterly deceived his excellent and simple employer, Mr. Colvend ; he had been insolent to Mr. Surlees ; he had declined the chaste pleasures, the intellectual converse, of Mr. Colvend's house, and descended to the lowest social stratum to be found even in London. He had consorted with thieves and vagabonds ; he had gone into their haunts, and treated them with gin. One of the frater-

nity who called at his lodgings, had been
invited to partake of mild refreshment,
which assumed the character of brandy
in its integrity. He (the learned counsel)
was aware an endeavour would be made to
explain away these and other awkward
facts; but the overpowering evidence on
the part of the firm must render all such
efforts worse than useless. To see a man
of parts—a gentleman by birth, education,
association—one who, favoured by Nature
and caressed by Fortune, might have
hoped to climb to the highest rung of the
world's ladder—standing, like the common
felons with whom he had consorted, in the
dock, wrung his (the learned counsel's)
heart—at which point the learned counsel
thumped that organ. But he had a duty
to perform, and he meant to perform it, without fear and without favour, just as he knew
the intelligent jury he had the privilege to
address would perform theirs, regardless of

ridicule, undaunted by calumny, undeterred
by the false, though amiable, representa-
tions of the prisoner's too partial friends.

Stripped of its verbiage, the whole
speech, which did not occupy above fifteen
minutes in its delivery, was absurd in the
extreme—so absurd that Mr. Gayre could
see even the prisoner's lip quiver under
his close moustache ("Hang him!"
thought the banker; "this poor dog
whose day is ended has a sense of
humour"); but it told. Old Bailey juries
and the learned counsel were old and
fast friends. If jurors never exactly understood the barrister, the barrister understood jurors.

"They don't want much," he explained,
in the easy confidence of private life,
"but they do like it uncommonly strong.
Pitch into a man, give it him right and
left, and you get a verdict. Mistakes!
Bless your innocence" (only the learned

counsel employed a stronger phrase), " a judge of the realm can't make a mistake. If a man is not ripe for hanging to-day you may feel very sure he will be over-ripe next year; and it is better to garner the criminal crop early rather than late; that is all." And, strongly convinced the Oliver Dane crop was ready for the sickle, the learned counsel hitched up his robe, settled his wig firmly on his head as though a thunderstorm were impending, and " went for " that ungrateful young gentleman with a fury and acrimony which would have delighted those writers for the press who denounced the Cato Street con-spirators. He, the learned counsel, meant to show twelve honest men what an unmi-tigated and irredeemable scoundrel the prisoner at the bar really was. And then he proceeded to examine Mr. Surlees, who was the first witness called on behalf of the prosecution; while Susan Drummond spoke no word, and turned no look towards her companions, though Mr. Gayre could see she dug the fingers of one hand into the palm of the other till it bled ; then she began as of deliberate intent and tore her handkerchief into strips. The banker beckoned his servant, who stood not far off, and handed the man a leaf from his pocket-book. During the course of that trial Susan all unwittingly tore five handkerchiefs and a fan to tatters, festooned her watch-chain into loops till she broke it, slit her gloves beyond the possibility of further use, and picked the whole of the fringe off one side of her mantle.

A sadly untrained young woman ! If Sir Geoffrey had been going to the scaffold Miss Chelston would have adjusted every frill and tucker, fastened her brooch, smoothed her hair, and rubbed her eyes into a state of touching redness, ere descending to receive the condolences of her friends.

After all, it must be a great trial to people who believe these and such-like items compass temporal salvation to meet with persons who do not.

Mr. Surlees, judging from his evidence, seemed to be a man who was at one in his opinions with Miss Chelston. He had never thought Dane a business sort of young man; he considered he was too fond of new-fashioned ways. Mr. Colvend being infatuated about their clerk, he deemed it only his duty to warn his partner he did not believe Dane could ever become a fitting person to take into the house. He had received more than one warning about the prisoner— half a dozen, perhaps, in all. They assumed the shape of anonymous letters. He could form no idea from whom they emanated. In consequence, he examined the books. He found some discrepancies in them; he was intending to ask Dane to explain, when his attention was called to the fact of a cheque being missing. His suspicions at once fell on the prisoner. He spoke to his partner, who wanted to speak to Dane. Instead of speaking to Dane, however, a detective was sent for. The detective proceeded to the clerk's lodgings, where the notes, with which the cheque was cashed at the Union, were found in his portmanteau, packed as if ready for a journey.

Being cross-examined by Mr. Tirling, the prisoner's counsel, Mr. Surlees was entreated to describe his idea of a business young man. Mr. Tirling convulsed the court, always ready to laugh at nothing, but did no good to his client. The airy and humorous way in which this learned counsel delighted in putting things, in slyly chaffing his learned friend, poking fun at the judge, and driving Mr. Surlees to the verge of distraction, amused but did not convince twelve " conscientious, impartial and intelligent men."

Mr. Tirling wanted to know more than Mr. Clennam ever thought of, when he went to the Circumlocution Office. The learned counsel commenced operations with requiring a definition of a business sort of young man—not too fond of new-fashioned ways. Finding Mr. Surlees incapable of putting his notions into the concrete, he asked all sorts of questions concerning the model or dream young man. Mr. Surlees turning sulky at a very early stage of these proceedings, and the judge interposing with a remark that he did not really think the learned counsel's questions had the smallest bearing on the point at issue, Mr. Tirling argued the matter out with his lordship, and, being practically granted permission to ask such questions as he liked proceeded to inquire whether Mr. Surlees took Charles Lamb's good clerk as his model.

"I think all C. Lamb's clerks very excellent; I only wish we had a few like them," was the unexpected reply. Whereupon, said the newspaper reports, the court was convulsed, the fact being the laughter was confined entirely to the bench and the bar.

"Mr Surlees' acquaintance with Elia does not appear to have been intimate," suggested his lordship, wiping his wise old eyes. Whereupon there ensued a smart little dialogue between the bench and the learned counsel concerning Lamb and Leadenhall Street, Talfourd and the Inner Temple, which might have seemed more agreeable to the prisoner had he been unaware the discussion could not possibly influence his fate for good or for evil, that, forgetting all this pleasant fooling, the judge would eventually sum up dead against Oliver Dane!

Mr. Tirling inquired whether Mr. Dane wrote a "fair and swift hand," whether he was clean and neat in his person, whether he kept his books fair and unblemished, whether, in the mornings, he was first at the desk, whether he was temperate, whether he avoided profane oaths and jesting, whether the colour of his clothes was generally black in preference to brown, and brown rather than blue and green. And finding Mr. Surlees unable to answer any of these queries in the negative, the learned counsel suddenly dropped his friendly and conversational manner, and demanded with great sternness what further or higher qualities he could wish in a clerk.

Driven to bay Mr. Surlees answered,

"Honesty, for instance."

"That won't do," retorted the learned counsel.   "You   conceived   a prejudice

against my unfortunate client long before
any doubt concerning his honesty crossed
your mind. Remember you are on your
oath, sir. Now what was your particular objection to Mr. Dane?"

It was like applying the thumbscrew torture, and Mr. Surlees stammered out that
he thought their clerk talked too much,
and was a fop.

Instantly Mr. Tirling smote the witness
hip and thigh.

"Did Mr. Surlees know the meaning
attached to fop?"

"Yes, Mr. Surlees thought he did."

"Would he be kind enough to explain?"

Mr. Surlees declined this challenge.
"There were," he said, "words the meaning of which could not be explained by the
help of other words."

"There are, are there?" retorted Mr.
Tirling; and straightway begged his lordship to take a note of this reply.

Instead of doing anything of the sort,
his lordship said he thought the learned
gentleman was travelling very wide of the
subject indeed; to which remark the
learned gentleman replied his lordship would
ere long, comprehend the reason for the
course he was taking, and with all due
submission begged to state he felt if he
were to do justice to the prisoner—than
whom no more cruelly maligned individual
ever deserved the sympathy of his fellow-
creatures—he must be allowed to continue
the cross-examination in his own way. The
judge gave consent by silence. The oppos-
ing counsel looked up at the ceiling, and
smiled as one who should say, " Let him
have his fling. It is all of no use; but he
must do something for his money." The
prisoner knew if his chances had been bad
ten minutes previously they were worse
now. With all the veins of his heart he
wished he had employed no solicitor,

secured no counsel, but just let things drift.

What was the loneliness of his prison cell in comparison with this idiotic splitting of hairs, and attempt to make a man out a liar who, to the best of his knowledge stood there trying to tell the simple truth?

" Now attend to me, sir, if you please ; " it was Mr. Tirling who spoke this sentence. " On your oath, do you consider Oliver Dane to be a person of weak understanding and much ostentation? O, you don't ? You are quite sure of that? Very well. Do you believe it was his ambition to attract attention by showy dress and pertness? Certainly not. Thank you, Mr. Surlees ; I thought we should get at something after a time. Did he strike you as a gay, trifling man? Once again, no. I trust these answers will be remembered. Was he, then, a coxcomb or a popinjay? Again No. Now really this is very sin-

gular. You described Mr. Dane as a fop
yet when one comes to exhaust the matter it actually seems he has not a single
fop-like quality. Perhaps the other cause
of dislike was founded on equally unsub-
stantial grounds. You say, sir, Mr. Dane
talked too much; why, even Charles
Lamb's model clerk was permitted the
occasional use of his tongue. What did
Mr. Dane say, when did he say it, and
how? O, you decline to answer! Well,
let that pass. Now I want to know who
called your attention to the fact that a
cheque had been torn out of the book?"

With this question Mr. Surlees tried in
vain to fence; Mr. Tirling was determined
he would—as he unpleasantly expressed the
matter—" have an answer out of him," and
at length elicited that Mr. Surlees was the
Columbus of this great discovery; that he
had " called his own attention " to it.

Then, indeed, the learned counsel felt

delighted. In the playful exuberance of his
spirits he figuratively danced round and
round the merchant, dealing him verbal
blows, catching him with a jest and gibe
under the fifth rib; getting him into a
corner, and making him contradict himself half a dozen times in as many seconds;
closing with him as if for a mighty tussle;
and then at quite an unexpected moment
intimating in a scornful manner he had done
with him.

This might have been all very well had
his ingenuity proved able to tell the jury
how notes paid across the counter of the
Union on one day came, on the next evening,
to be found in Mr. Dane's possession. It
was a circumstance which of course might
be capable of explanation; but then neither
Mr. Dane nor Mr. Dane's counsel managed
to do anything of the sort. The notes had
been sent to him, so said the prisoner; the
parcel containing them was dropped into the

letter-box of his lodgings, the only information which accompanied it being that they
came "from a friend." Certainly such a
story did not seem feasible. It was just
within the bounds of possibility that it might
be true; but then it was so much more
probable that it might not. Incredulity was
writ large on the faces of those twelve men
with whom the result lay. There are things
that cannot be got over save by faith, a
quality for which the British juryman is not
usually remarkable; and if he had ever
possessed it in the case of Oliver Dane, it
may safely be said every step of the trial,
every fact extracted in cross-examination
and from the witnesses produced for the
defence, must have tended to weaken the
conviction of Oliver Dane's innocence.

There never seemed a clearer case of
heartless ingratitude and flagrant fraud.

On the part of Mr. Colvend, at all events,
there could be no suspicion of prejudice or

dislike. Every answer he gave clearly proved his affection for the prisoner—his grief and surprise when he heard of the accusation against him; yet his evidence, reluctantly given, could only be summed up as against Oliver Dane. Had the matter rested with him, the young man would not have been given into custody; but that he believed in his guilt was evident. He knew he was going into business on his own account, and had offered to assist him; would gladly have lent him three hundred pounds or more had he been aware such a sum was important. Not a word was said or sentence spoken during the whole course of the trial which did not make the case blacker against the criminal.

"He ought to have pleaded guilty," thought Mr. Gayre. "Chelston was quite right; every fresh scrap of evidence is an additional nail in his coffin. Even *she* must be convinced now;" and he looked down at Susan, who, raising her anxious eyes, whispered, as if in answer to his unspoken words,

"Remember all this does not change my opinion in the least. He is innocent. I do not expect you to think so, but I know it."

The end was nearly at hand. Sir Geoffrey Chelston, who had been intimate with all the Danes—Oliver included—came forward to state he believed Dane to be a most honourable fellow, one he had never seen but once on any racecourse. Pressed as to whether the prisoner was not fond of horses, he answered, "Of course; all gentlemen are;" which last assertion might as well have been omitted, if he wished to impress the jury with any idea of the advantages to be derived from his own acquaintance. There was only one witness whose testimony could have proved useful on behalf of the prisoner; but both Mr. Gayre and Oliver Dane had so managed that her name was not even known to Mr. Tirling.

" Wouldn't do, you know, Gayre," remarked Sir Geoffrey, talking the matter over with his brother-in-law. " Susan must not be mixed up publicly with that poor fellow's troubles. Besides, nothing can materially change the aspect of matters for him ; it is a mere question of so many months, more or less ; and what can a few months more or less signify to him? while it would be perfect damnation—excuse the word—for the girl to be bracketed with a fellow residing, even temporarily, in one of her Majesty's gaols."

" And, at the most, all she could say is he might have had her money without ever asking for it," answered Mr. Gayre. " We must keep her out of the matter. It is a redeeming point in Dane that he seems more anxious by far about her than himself."

"So he ought to be. Hang the fellow! what business had he to induce such a girl to engage herself to a pauper? Now the only amends he can make is to leave her free to marry somebody else."

"She won't do that, I think," said Mr. Gayre, a little hypocritically.

"Won't she! Leave her to Time for a while. Old Time is the only fellow that thoroughly understands women. He heals love wounds, and turfs over graves, and dries up tears in a way you would scarcely credit. 'Pon my soul, I've known him work miracles, and so you'll find it with Sue; only whatever you do, don't cross her fancies," finished the Baronet, who already looked on Susan as Mrs. Gayre, and the Lombard Street strong-room as unlocked for his benefit.

It was, therefore, more with an interested eye to the future than from any sympathy with the unfortunate lovers that Sir Geoffrey worked for Oliver Dane as " though he were my own son."

Nevertheless, spite of the fact that he was a baronet, his testimony told, in the minds of the jury, against Mr. Colvend's clerk ; and not even the circumstance, that in cross-examination, to the great satisfaction of every one, the judge included, he threw the learned counsel for the prosecution, could make things better for a man accused of robbing his employers. Sir Geoffrey was quite sure of two things— one, that Oliver Dane did not bet ; another, that he did not habitually attend races.

"I'd know a betting-man," declared the Baronet, " if he were a bishop, or came on the course in wig and gown. I never saw Dane on any race-ground but once, and that was at the Derby, with a lot of other young fellows like himself. More by token," he added, nodding his head, and looking with a malicious twinkle at the learned counsel, "that was the very same year you laid against Bluegown, and lost a pot of money. I never shall forget your face when the roar came, 'Bluegown, Bluegown!'"

There was such a laugh over this agreeable reminiscence that the judge's admonitions to Sir Geoffrey were quite unheard; and the Baronet, dismissed by his opponent, who desired no continuation of so unpleasant a tale, lounged easily out of the witness-box, before it dawned on anyone his lordship was remonstrating with him concerning the impropriety of his conduct.

After Sir Geoffrey came Lionel Hilderton, who was called to prove he and Oliver Dane had gone together into the low haunts of London in order to study faces and find models likely to prove useful in connection with his own work. They had found their way into very questionable neighbourhoods, and treated persons who were very like blackguards and thieves; but if they had what then? "No doubt you"—this pointedly, and in his most offensive manner, to the genial gentleman who was badgering him—"have, in the way of your trade, consorted, ere now, with bad characters. You would be very much offended, I dare-say, if anyone called you a pickpocket because you may have defended one."

"Such license of language really cannot be permitted," observed the judge.

"Then why," asked Lal, his dark eyes flashing with anger, "does your lordship allow that person such license of language in addressing me? It is hard to get a blow and not to have a chance of striking out in return;" following on which remark there ensued a very pretty little quarrel between bench and witness. Lal defied the judge, and the judge threatened to commit him. Lal said he did not care, and that, on the whole, he would rather be committed;

and it was at length only through the
interposition of the learned counsel engaged
on both sides his lordship was pacified, and
the young man induced to hold his tongue,
and the cross-examination proceeded.

"Were you ever engaged in a fight with
the police?" asked his persecutor.

"Yes, and I'd fight them again if they
were insolent. What right had they to
interfere with a man who was doing them
no harm?"

"Do you not think it was wrong to go
to such places as the police warned you
were not fit for any decently-dressed person
to enter?"

"No, not a bit more wrong than going to
church," retorted Lal.

"Perhaps you don't go to church, Mr.
Hilderton?"

"Yes, I do, to study the British
Pharisee."

"Dear—dear—dear!" murmured Susan,

in an agony, wringing her hands; "what madness could have induced them to call Lal?"

"He has done all that lay in his power to convict his friend," decided Mr. Gayre. but he did not utter this idea aloud. "Won't you come away now, Miss Drummond?" he entreated, for he knew the beginning of the end was at hand.

"No; O, no!" she murmured.

"I wish you would not stop, dear," said Miss Matthews.

"I must stay to hear—the worst," Susan almost whispered.

Still the dreary proceedings dragged their slow length along; but at last came the judge's summing-up. It was dead against the prisoner, who stood listening, with crossed arms and an unmoved front, to the words of wisdom and reprobation which flowed in smooth passionless accents from the bench. The question of the prisoner's

guilt or innocence, was left, of course, to
the jury; but the jury were told how to
decide. The crime of which the young
man before them was accused struck at
the foundations of society. It was for the
jury to disembarrass their minds of the
extraneous matters which had been obtruded
on their notice, and deliver a verdict on
the merits of the case. His lordship felt he
need not remind the gentlemen of the jury
that the fact of the prisoner being well born,
well educated, well connected, could not
palliate his sin, if they believed he had first
stolen a cheque, then forged his employers'
signature, and subsequently appropriated the
proceeds. It was for the jury to say whether
they considered this serious charge proved.

Apparently, the jury had arrived at their
decision before they even left the box; for
they were not ten minutes absent before
they trooped back again solemnly. They
had arrived at a verdict.

" How say you, gentlemen ? "

And then Susan Drummond, though she knew what was coming, held her breath.

" *Guilty !* "

It seemed as if a thousand voices took up the word, and shouted it in her ears. For a moment she felt like one drowning ; the waters had indeed covered her soul.

" Let me take you out," said Mr. Gayre, touching her arm ; but she seemed not to hear him. Every sense was concentrated on the judge, who, in measured accents, proceeded to say he would not add to the distress the prisoner must feel at the position to which a long course of folly and extravagance had brought him. When he looked back over his wasted life—a life which he could so easily have made honourable and prosperous—it might well seem as if in the loss of the esteem of all honest men, in the wreck and ruin of his own career, in the reproaches of his own conscience, were the elements of a sufficient and terrible punishment; but the crime of which a jury of his own countrymen had found him guilty, was one so dangerous to the community, so necessary to check in a vast city—the capital of the greatest mercantile nation in the world, or that the world had ever known—his lordship felt it necessary to pass the severe sentence of seven years' penal servitude.

"My God!" exclaimed the prisoner, like one stunned; and at that moment Susan would have risen, but that Mr. Gayre prevented her from doing so.

"Don't make a scene," he entreated, "don't;" while from the dock came a cry of "*I am innocent!*" ere the warders hurried the living man into the seven years' grave that yawned before him.

CHAPTER IX.

"EVENTS ARRANGE THEMSELVES."

"SEVEN years, by Jove!" said Sir Geoffrey, pacing the length and breadth of Mr. Gayre's dining-room, his head sunk on his breast, his hands clasped behind his back. "Seven years! Good God Almighty!" and the Baronet, in a vague sort of way, fell to considering what he, Geoffrey Chelston, could have made of seven long years spent in penal servitude, had the Gayres dealt with him "according to law."

"Seven years without drink or dice or pretty barmaids—without flats or cheats, or horses or racecourses—with no society save the dumb company of those who had been 'found out'—with the shape of his head and ears too painfully defined—clad in a suit for which no tailor could ever dun him—forced to go to bed with that silly creature the lamb, and compelled to rise with that greater nuisance and greater fool still the lark—obliged to go to church, and knuckle down to the chaplain, and eat, begad, any beastly stuff a rascally Radical Government elected to thrust down the throat of gentlemen in trouble—a damned lot!"

Thus the tenth Baronet, who had put his name and ancestry and title and money out to such extraordinary interest, stung into mental activity by the fact of so severe a sentence being passed upon a man who had not shaved the wind one whit closer than himself, regarded the "might have been" of his own case, while ostensibly considering the sore plight of that "unlucky devil," Oliver Dane.

"It all comes of keeping a fellow too tight," went on the Baronet, talking to Mr.

Gayre as though the banker were an utter tyro in the ways of this wicked but pleasant old world. " A man must have his fling sometime, and if he hasn't it early he'll take it late. 'Pon my soul, I'm as sorry for Dane as if he were my own brother! It's a deuced hard case. I am sure I said all I could for him. Had he been my father I couldn't have sworn harder, and yet I feel as though I were in some sort to blame—as if I might have said more, you know. I declare, Gayre, to my dying day I shall never forget his cry, ' I am innocent ! ' "

" But he was not innocent," objected Mr. Gayre.

" I am not so sure of that : standing almost in the presence of his Maker, as one may say ; for seven years' penal servitude in this world appears to me far more like eternity, and a very bad eternity, than walking over the border into a land the parsons seem to think will be made pleasant for most of us who are not hardened and desperate ruffians—a well-connected and respectable young fellow like Dane—Heavens! I remember him quite a little lad running about in knickerbockers—would be scarcely likely to tell a lie."

"No one could have felt more sure of his guilt than yourself," said the banker, angrily; "what is the use of talking in this strain now?"

"None—not a bit; and that's just what makes me take the whole thing so much to heart. Innocent or guilty, such a sentence is enough to make a man, if he had not the very strongest faith—which, thank God! I have—turn atheist. Seven years cut clean out of a fellow's life! Better have hung him at once. Could that old fool of a judge understand what seven years of penal servitude means to a gentleman well born, well bred, well connected? I feel as if I'd like to go and assault somebody—I might get the case ventilated then. And then there's poor dear Susan breaking her soft tender heart ; and, as I told her this morning, I am only able to stand like a brute and do nothing ; and then what d'ye think she did ? "

" Thanked you for your sympathy, I have no doubt."

"She never said a word. She just came up to me, and put her arms round my neck and kissed me, and laid her pretty head on my shoulder and cried like a child. I'm a rough and tumble sort of chap, and nobody ever suggested there was any gammon or sentiment about Geoffrey Chelston ; but, upon my soul, Gayre,"—and the unsentimental Baronet, instead of finishing his sentence, fetched a deep breath—" A woman like Susan Drummond can make what she will of a man," he went on, " hand in hand with her, a fellow need never wish to wander out of that path to heaven which we are told is so confoundedly narrow and straight."

"I never heard the path was straight," remarked Mr. Gayre, "though I fancy many persons find it so."

"Hang it all, you need not take me up so short! Besides, I gave the spirit of the text, and surely that's enough. And as for Susan, narrow or straight, or both, she'd lead the worst sinner that ever lived to the happy land school-children sing about. Faith, it was very pretty to hear them at Chelston, Gayre; poor Margaret used—"

"Miss Drummond does not seem to have been able to lead her particular sinner to a very happy land, in this world, at all events," said Mr. Gayre, ruthlessly cutting across his brother-in-law's pastoral reminiscences.

"Now don't be ironical," entreated Sir Geoffrey.

"Ironical! Good gracious!"

"Well, ironical, or sarcastic, or what you

choose, you were sneering at Dane, you
know you were, and it's not kind to sneer
at a fellow who has got into hot water and
been badly scalded."

"I don't know what you mean," returned
Mr. Gayre. "I suppose we have all a right
to express an opinion, and when a man
embezzles and forges—"

"Well, you need not be hard on him ;
and you are much harder than I like to see—
you are, Gayre, upon my conscience."

"And upon *my* conscience," retorted the
banker, "I utterly fail to understand the
drift of all your profound remarks. It is
impossible in the face of the evidence you
heard yesterday for you, or any man, to
believe Dane innocent, and being guilty he
deserves punishment. Seven years is a heavy
sentence, no doubt, but employers *must* be
protected. Supposing you left your purse on
that table, and a housemaid stole it, would
you give her a sovereign and entreat her to

remain in your service? You know you would not; you would send for the nearest policeman and give her in charge—"

"I'd do nothing of the sort," interrupted the Baronet. "She should never have a chance of robbing me again, but—"

"You would give her a chance to rob somebody else," suggested Mr. Gayre.

"I'd rather do that than lock her up," said Sir Geoffrey, standing to his guns. "I do not believe in all this law and lawyer business, and punishing and deterring and the rest of it. If a fellow goes wrong, give him a chance of doing right. How can any one get right working like a navvy at Portland? Supposing those two City Solons had left Dane free, and let him repay their money, it would have been better for everybody, themselves included."

"In that case, he might have married Miss Drummond, and lived happily ever after," sneered Mr. Gayre.

"I shouldn't have gone so far as that," answered the Baronet. " And, indeed, I doubt if Susan would have wished to marry him ; now she does ; that's the first effect of his lordship's sentence. The girl considers her lover a martyr, which brings me to what I particularly wanted to say. For Heaven's sake, Gayre, don't hurt her feelings by speaking as if you thought him guilty ! If you do, she'll hate you for ever. There is no manner of use in reasoning with a woman—women can't reason any more than they can grill a steak. Let Susan have her way. If she likes to believe Dane innocent, it won't do you or me any harm. Soothing is the way to treat such a wound. If any likely young fellow were about, now would be his chance ; no time for winning a girl's heart so good as when it has just been broken, and while her eyes are still wet with crying ! Gad ! I mayn't know much about the business world and

money and so forth, but I do understand
women! Though I am not as young as I
used to be, if I were single I'd engage to
have Susan Drummond for wife in three
months."

"Upon the whole it is fortunate for her
that you are not single," remarked Mr.
Gayre.

"O, I don't mean to say that I should
wish to marry Susan," returned Sir Geoffrey;
"only that I know I could. We should
not suit each other in the least. I'd drive
her mad; and she — well, fact is, Susan
would be a bit too good for me. She
ought to run in harness with some steady
fellow, who does not drink or gamble, who
has not been driven half mad with trouble,
and compelled to pick up a wretched living
as I am. I'd like to see her married to
some excellent man she could be proud of
—rich, respectable, that sort of thing; what
I never can be now, Gayre. It would be

an awful business if she made a mistake
a second time. Just fancy her tied for
life to a sulky beggar like Lal Hilderton,
or to such an infernal cad as your friend
Sudlow!" Having planted which sting in
his brother-in-law's soul, Sir Geoffrey walked
to the side-board, and refreshed himself
with about half a tumbler of Chartreuse
that had been produced for his especial
benefit, as he said he felt deucedly queer,
and could think of nothing so likely to
pull him together a bit.

"I don't know what I am to do with
Sudlow," he began, after partaking of this
moderate draught. "He's as shy of those
settlements as if they were a ten-foot wall.
I bring him up to them again and again,
but he always refuses the leap. Now it's
this, now it's the other; something has
been left out, or something has been put
in. He goes to my lawyers: for I can't
have him bothering me, and he won't, he

declares, incur the expense of letting his own solicitor arrange the matter—I am sure he is afraid the attorney would sell him—goes to my lawyers, and argues each point with them. Heaven only knows who is to pay the piper. I know I sha'n't be able."

"And I really don't think Sudlow will," said Mr. Gayre.

"Things are getting deucedly awkward. I must give up Moreby's crib ere long. His mother's legal adviser says I may rent the place on, if I choose to pay in advance, but that he cannot advise his client to permit the present unsatisfactory arrangements to continue, and be blanked to him. Then I am all at sea as to what I am to do about Maggie. Clearly Sudlow mustn't be hanging round the house while the girl is alone in it; and I can't be mewed up in North Bank for ever. If I am to stop at home all day, the pot would soon cease

boiling. You must see yourself it is of no
earthly use trying to get 'companions;' they
won't stop; money won't make them—love
might. I believe old mother Morris expected
I would propose for her. It's deucedly awkward, confoundedly awkward. I've looked
at the position from, I think, every possible
and impossible point of view, and the more
I think the more satisfied I feel there is
but one course open, and that is making
things up with Margaret."

"Well, of course, you know your own
business best," said Mr. Gayre, who understood whither all this was tending.

"There are few men who would propose
such a plan," said Sir Geoffrey, helping himself to a little more Chartreuse; "but I
do not profess to be led by popular opinion.
My notions are not worldly, but I hope
they are Christian. Dear, dear, when I look
back to the old times, and think of Margaret and the Pleasaunce! Ah! she was a

lovely young creature, Gayre, and nobody can deny the Pleasaunce was as sweet a spot as ever a set of rascally Jews got hold of! Lord! when I shut my eyes I can see her standing beside one of the windows in the great drawing-room at Chelston, framed in a tracery of leaves and roses, the red in her cheeks pink as the roses, and her forehead white as her dress. The fairest picture: the quaint old furniture and the sweet young bride. Ah, the house is dismantled, and Margaret gone! Many a man has hung himself for less, Gayre."

"It is not a particularly agreeable theme for Margaret's brother," observed the banker.

"Rough on you," agreed Sir Geoffrey, "deucedly rough. Hard for me—harder for you. Impossible to wash such a stain clean out of any family; and to think that the cowardly fellow escaped without having to pay even a farthing damages!"

"It would not have benefited Margaret

much if he had," said Mr. Gayre, who knew into whose pocket the damages would have found their way.

"The more I think over the matter, the more satisfied I feel Peggy and her mother ought to be together," declared Sir Geoffrey, ignoring his brother-in-law's remark.

Mr. Gayre also was aware when it was prudent to maintain silence, and discreetly held his peace.

"Have you thought over what I said to you a little while since?" asked the Baronet, finding this astute fish declined to "rise."

"What did you say? Put your idea into plain words."

"You might help a man a little, more especially when he is making such an offer as I am making now. Hang it! if Margaret were *my* sister, and *you*, her wronged husband, were proposing to let bygones be bygones, and have her back, you could not take things more coolly than you are doing."

" I do not feel elated, if that is what you mean," said Mr. Gayre.

" Well, of all the cold, bloodless fellows I ever met," Sir Geoffrey was beginning, when a look, in the banker's face warned him to desist. " We can't be *all* alike, however," he added in a tone of bland apology for the fact.

" We can't all be Geoffrey Chelstons if that is what you mean," agreed the banker.

" We can't be all Gayres either. Gad, in many ways I wish we could. But now to revert to Margaret. You would like the past to be forgotten, eh ? "

" It cannot be undone."

" That's true ; but where's the use of harping upon that ? It would gratify you to know your sister had resumed her old position and rank, and so forth, eh ? "

" I don't know that it would. There is an

old proverb about letting sleeping dogs lie. Were Margaret to return to England, many sleeping dogs in the country would wake up and begin snarling at her."

"O no, they wouldn't. Scarce a soul ever knew the rights of that affair. I am sure, Gayre, even you must say no man could have kept stricter silence than I."

"Whatever your reason may have been for holding your tongue, I never found fault with you for doing so," returned Mr. Gayre, dryly.

"That's City all over. I wonder if you would have made such a speech while you were in the thick of the dashing fellows who saved India for us? But never mind, I know you better than you know yourself, and feel quite sure business has not really spoiled one I can remember as generous and trustful and enthusiastic a young man as ever wore her Majesty's uniform."

Mr. Gayre did not answer this bitter-sweet

encomium. Once again Sir Geoffrey had touched the raw, as that worthy understood.

" Well, well," he said, " we can't be hard hearted men of the world, and keep the soft tender hearts of boyhood in our breasts, too. Still, thank Heaven, all I have gone through has not made me cast iron. I can't forget, though you do. I wish we could have been more like brothers, Gayre. I'm an unfortunate devil, I know ; but I always was fond of you, and misfortune is not crime. I did think you would be pleased at my notion about Margaret—poor misguided soul! However, of course, I can't expect you to see with my eyes ; so Peggy and I must do the best we can for ourselves, and that best will be bad enough. Good-bye. Heaven only knows when I shall see you again. I hope you may always be prosperous, and never know what it is to hunger for a kind word or look, and get neither ; " with which Christian aspiration, that sounded uncommonly like a curse, Sir

Geoffrey was turning towards the door, when Mr. Gayre stopped him,

"Wait a moment, Chelston," he said. "Don't go yet."

The banker was standing before the fire, looking into its glowing depths, and did not see the smile which overspread Sir Geoffrey's face as he paused to ask,

"Well, what is it now?"

"That is what I wish to know," answered Mr. Gayre. "Why can't you tell me in so many plain words exactly what you want? If you know anything about me, you ought to understand the sort of talk in which you have been indulging is completely wasted. I despise flattery as much as I distrust sentimentality. You never liked one of us; you thought we might serve your turn. As for Margaret, a pert serving-wench would have found more favour in your eyes than my sister. I declare," added the banker, in a burst of fury, "when I think of all Margaret suffered at your hands, I hate myself for ever having crossed your threshold again, or eaten your bread, or let my hand touch yours in amity."

"You know I can't hit back, Gayre; and it really was deucedly good of you to forget old grievances—utterly imaginery, upon my soul—for the sake of Peggy."

A dull red line, like a band, came slowly across Mr. Gayre's forehead. Perhaps he was conscious of that tell-tale mark, for he never turned towards Sir Geoffrey as he answered,

"I would have done a good deal for my sister's daughter, but I find that daughter almost as impracticable and selfish as yourself. I don't know what can be done for her."

"Don't you? If you chose to give Peggy a fortune, no man would find her waste it in making presents, for example."

"But I *don't* choose to give her a fortune."

"I know you don't; you are far too like

her to do anything of the sort. I was only remarking, if you tried the experiment of giving Peggy any of this world's goods, you'd find she'd take deucedly good care of number one. She can make a pound go further than I could five. Faith! spite of her beauty and the long line of ancestry she is able to claim on my side, I often think it would be a pity to spoil two houses with her and Sudlow. There is a regular trade smack about the girl at times which positively amazes me. It just shows that what's bred in the bone, you know—"

"Where is all this tending?" interrupted Mr. Gayre.

"I don't know that it is tending anywhere except to lodgings at fifteen shillings a week and good-bye to Sudlow," answered Sir Geoffrey. "I had better be going, Gayre. I am confoundedly sorry I came."

"What is the amount of annual income over and above the sum I allow my sister

you require to set up house with Lady
Chelston at the head of affairs? Remember,
I promise nothing. I do not even know that
Margaret would return to you; if she did. I
fail to understand what is to be said to her
daughter concerning a mother she believes
died long and long ago. Still, I should like
to know your price; you came to tell me that
price; out with it, man."

"Well, as you force me to say, I think ten
thousand pounds down, and five hundred a
year for Margaret's and my life, at our death
to go then to Peggy, would be just to me and
not unfair to you."

"Just to *you!*" repeated Mr. Gayre.

"I don't expect you to think much about
the justice to me," replied Sir Geoffrey
equably. "Why should you? Why should
a rich man consider a poor one? Why
should you, who have always been first
favourite with Fortune, think for a moment
about an out-at-elbows fellow like myself.

The ball is at your foot, not at mine ; play it, knock me over! Only deal kindly with Margaret and the girl, and I am content to hang on to life by my eyelids as I am doing now, till a pauper's grave receives all that is mortal of the tenth Baronet of Chelston."

" As for ten thousand pounds down, I won't give you a thousand pence."

" Then I needn't detain you longer. I am sorry I mentioned the matter at all, only I thought and still think Margaret is the proper person to take charge of her child. No one but a mother can see to a girl, and I'd have made things as pleasant as possible. I'd have stopped out of her way except when it was necessary for me to enter an appearance. I'd have left Margaret and **Peggy** to manage matters just as they liked, and only put in a word if asked to do so. You and your sister could have selected a residence to suit her; bless you! though I make no fuss or pretence, I'm full of consideration. I'd have left her as free as air. If she ever wanted to ask a few friends, she could have sent out the invitations as if from Sir Geoffrey and Lady Chelston; and I'd have come up to time. Of course I understood, after the way she had treated me, she might feel more comfortable if I were not constantly at hand to remind her of the past. Poor dear soul! She couldn't help being a simpleton, I daresay, but still—"

"Sir Geoffrey, will you have the kindness to leave my house?"

Mr. Gayre was almost beside himself with rage.

"Certainly, certainly," answered Sir Geoffrey, with the greatest equanimity. "If you don't mind, I'll just have another sip of that Chartreuse, and then I'll be off."

"Finish the bottle if you like," said Mr.

Gayre, who knew the Baronet was certain
to do so without his permission.

"Thankee, I will; there's not much
left;" and Sir Geoffrey, having exactly
filled his tumbler with the precious liquor,
and, in an easy affable way, drained its
contents to the last drop, nodded to Mr.
Gayre and walked out of the room. Next
moment, however, he reappeared.

"I say, Gayre," he began, putting his
remarkable head inside the door, "you've
treated me deucedly badly to-day, I consider; but still, hang it, if blood is thicker
than water, a brother-in-law is a brother-
in-law; so I thought I'd just come back
and give you a bit of a hint. It's not
very likely you'll ever see Peggy again—
for I'm sure your friend the cad, upon
whom we've wasted such a lot of valuable
time, will never be got over that rasping
settlement fence, and I'll have to start
the girl out as nursery governess or lady-

help, or something of that sort—still if you ever should, don't tell her that you think Dane guilty. Though she is my daughter, she's as nasty and venomous a little toad as ever held the making of a truly respectable and conventional woman. She'd tell Susan instantly. Poor Susan! Now, there is breed. The Drummonds never married beneath them—never."

"Not even into the Mrs. Arbery clique," suggested Mr. Gayre.

Sir Geoffrey was out on the doorstep ere the banker had got half through this sentence, and before it ended had crossed the street and was sauntering along the kerb, shaking his head with repressed delight, and smiling to such an extent, the few persons he met turned to look back after his retreating figure.

"That sprat will catch that herring," he decided. "I'll screw fifteen hundred perhaps out of him, and he'll make Mar-

garet's allowance a thousand a year. It
will be a wonderful relief to me. I shan't
then care a snap of my fingers whether
Sudlow marries Peggy or not; I should
never be a penny the better if she did."

Sir Geoffrey's spirit of prophecy proved
in many respects correct. Mr. Gayre's first
determination was, indeed, to sever the
whole connection; but eventually calmer
thought prevailed. He could not blind
himself to the truth that it would be making the best of a bad business to adopt
his brother-in-law's suggestion, and place
"Peg" under her mother's care. He had
no intention of paying a large sum in
order to effect the needful reconciliation,
but he would be willing to pay something.
It was easy enough to resume outwardly
friendly relations with Sir Geoffrey, who
never took offence unless he meant to make
a profit by doing so. A hint was given
to Lady Chelston of the happiness which

might be in store; and had her husband
been the best man living, she could scarcely
have expressed greater thankfulness for his
generosity or more fervent hope that nothing
might occur to prevent the proposed
arrangement being carried out. Sir Geoffrey walked jauntily about London with
so jubilant a manner people imagined he
must have had a fortune left to him. Even
Mr. Sudlow began to feel satisfied some
extraordinary piece of luck had fallen in
the Baronet's way, and yielded a point in
the settlements, over which there had been
ceaseless wrangling. Mrs. Moreby's lawyer
and several rather pressing creditors were
quieted and satisfied without that awkward
business the exchange of money, and things
seemed to be going almost—to quote Sir
Geoffrey's own words—"too smooth," when
one evening while he was sitting over his
wine with a few choice spirits he had
invited to a "quiet dinner and rubber to

follow," Lavender appeared, carrying a telegram on one of Mr. Moreby's salvers.

Unwitting of evil, the Baronet cut open
the envelope, and with a bland " Excuse
me," read:

" *Margaret died this afternoon, very suddenly. I start for France by night mail.*"

" Talk about Job!" thought Sir Geoffrey;
but, with suppressed and creditable emotion,
he said aloud, " This," and he touched the
telegram, " announces the death of one very
near and dear to me. Gentlemen, will you
excuse me, and make yourselves at home?
I shall just have time to catch the express
to Dover. Lavender, a hansom, quick, with
a horse that can go. O, I have no gold!
Can anybody lend me five pounds? Thank
you, very much."

And the Baronet was gone to bid good-
bye to Peggy.

CHAPTER X.

THE WIDOWER.

AT his wife's funeral Sir Geoffrey developed quite a new accomplishment. HE WEPT! Circumstances had kept him compulsorily sober; and sobriety did what brandy never could have done—made him maudlin. Mr. Gayre did not believe in his brother-in-law's tears, yet he felt touched by them. They fell like rain; they were to be seen of all men. The undertaker, who knew his money to be safe, was quite affected, and afterwards spoke of Sir Geoffrey's emotion as "most creditable to all parties." In gloomy silence the Baronet thinking of what might have been and of what indeed was so near being, stood and

looked at the changed calm face of his once
beautiful wife. He could not have shed a
tear then—he explained that he felt turned
into stone—had the whole of the money in
Gayres' bank been offered to him as the
price of that precious crystal; but in the
watches of the night, which, contrary to
custom, he was forced to spend in bed,
" tossing and turning and burnt up with a
consuming thirst, begad!" he evolved a
brilliant idea, which he confided to his
brother-in-law next morning.

"Look here, Gayre," he began. "I
wonder why we can't have sensible break-
fasts like this in England, instead of that
eternal tea or coffee which plays the very
deuce with a man's nerves and digestion.
That is not what I was going to say to
you, though. I didn't get a wink of sleep
last night—couldn't sleep, you know. All
the past rushed back upon me like a wave
—well, well, it's no use talking about last

year's snow—and it came into my head
that you'd like to have Margaret laid at
Chelston. Of course everything is gone;
but I fancy I could manage that matter.
As for me, one place will be as good as
another—where the tree falls, you know (a
most inapt simile, because as a rule the
tree is never allowed to lie long anywhere).
But I do think if the poor girl could
speak, she would say, 'Lay me at Chelston!' Lord, when I think of her trotting
about at Christmastide, with a present for
this one and something for the other, I feel
as if my heart would break; I do, upon
my soul, Gayre!" And the Baronet
walked out of the room, ostensibly to hide
his emotion, but really to consider at
leisure the extent to which Mr. Gayre
would " fork out " for the glory and
privilege of having his sister buried
among " decent people."

There is an intuition, which seems to

be the exclusive birthright of dogs, children, women, fools, and scoundrels, that
serves its purpose better than any exhaus-
tive line of argument. This intuition Sir
Geoffrey possessed to its fullest extent, and
through it he understood his brother-in-
law would at length rise to the bait
offered. In good earnest Sir Geoffrey
could have made no proposition more
grateful to the banker's feelings. If Lady
Chelston were once laid to rest amongst
her husband's kindred, the world might
say its worst, and still be checkmated. If
Sir Geoffrey made the arrangements for
her funeral; if his friends attended it;
if he, for once, donning a black hat instead of a white one, appeared as chief
mourner, Mr. Gayre felt he could for ever
after snap his fingers in the face of Mrs.
Grundy. The best he had ever hoped was
to lay his poor erring and doubly-sinned-
against sister in some quiet grave in a

strange country and amongst a strange
people; but now the prospect opened
fairly amazed him. Of course he knew he
would have to pay in meal or in malt for
that niche in the Chelston vault; but he
was willing to pay for it. Sir Geoffrey
had touched everything that was weakest
and most vulnerable in his nature.

"Poor Margaret!—poor dear child! If
she could know, she would like it," he
thought; and the long years of trial and
shame and sorrow and seclusion faded
away from memory, and in fancy he once
again saw his little sister running races
with him up and down the stairs, and
along the halls and passages of his father's
house and the house occupied by Mr.
Higgs. He could hear the swish of the
stiffly-starched white dress, and the pitter-
patter of the tiny feet; behold once again
the flutter of a light-blue sash, and feel the
long curls touch his cheek, as, with a

laugh and a bound, she rushed out upon
him from some unsuspected ambuscade.

And there, still and cold, in an upper
chamber, lay all that remained of the
little sister grown to womanhood, who
had made what they all once thought so
great a match; who had suffered horribly
and sinned grievously, and repented in the
sackcloth of loneliness and the ashes of
isolation, and to whom he had not perhaps
been so kind as he might, and visited
less frequently than he cared to remember.
And life was over for her; and he could
have made it happier. And yes, certainly,
if it were possible to bring her to Chelston, she should lie there, though all the
stately matrons and discreet widows and
tender virgins mouldering to dust turned
in their coffins with righteous indignation
when this poor frail sinner was carried
into the last earthly home the portals of
which might ever open for her.

"You will want money," said Mr. Gayre
to the Baronet, whose chronic state it was
to stand in need of that necessary article.

But Sir Geoffrey knew when to hold his
hand as truly as he knew when to reap,
and at first refused to take the cheque Mr.
Gayre had already drawn.

"Leave it, leave it, my boy," he said,
with a spasm intended to act the manly
part of indicating the emotion he was
strong enough to repress; "time enough
to spare for all that when we know for
certain if our darling can rest where I
want to lay her. If I am able to do that
for her, I shan't feel so utterly miserable.
It's all I can try to do, Gayre. And now
I ought to be off at once. By the way,
d'ye happen to have any loose gold about
you? Lord, how money does sift away at
a time like this! No, no, no; I don't
want a twenty-pound note. Can't you give
me anything less?"

If Mr. Gayre could, he would not.

"Keep it," he said; "you don't know what you may need."

"Faith, no!" exclaimed Sir Geoffrey, struck by a sudden thought. "I had to borrow a fiver last night, or I couldn't have come. Well, good-bye, Gayre; and I'll wire you directly I have seen Wookes —that's the name of the fellow who has Chelston now."

"One moment. Don't you think— shouldn't you like—" suggested the dead woman's brother almost timidly.

"My dear fellow, a thousand thanks! I had forgotten—I had upon my soul— what might—what, indeed, must—happen before it would be possible for me to return. Poor, poor Margaret! poor sweet dear!" And the Baronet, who had earnestly hoped he might be spared another look at that face he never saw in life cold and statuesque, took off his hat, and laying

it on the table, lest he might, from sheer
force of habit, cover his head again even
in the death chamber ("which would play
the very devil," he considered), ran his
fingers through his hair, put on the most
solemn expression at his command—and
the Baronet's expression could not, as a
rule, be described as jocund—and inti-
mated to Mr. Gayre he was ready.

"Perhaps," said the banker, "you would
prefer to go upstairs alone."

"No, no, not at all. Why should not
we—the only two who seem to have cared
for her—stand beside her together? And
you know, Gayre, I *must* leave her to
your care."

As if, under any possible combination of
circumstances, Sir Geoffrey would have been
induced to remain sole, or indeed any,
guardian at all of the "poor pale" thing
laid helpless on its last bed upstairs!

In that sacred chamber the Baronet did

all, and indeed more than all, man could expect from man. He kissed the mask of life there stretched so stiff and stark; he touched the clay-cold hands; he severed, with the aid of a convenient pair of scissors—which, indeed, suggested the idea to him—a lock of hair once golden, but now plentifully sprinkled with gray.

"Lord, Lord!" said Sir Geoffrey, in severe expostulation with the Deity, "that we should come to this! On such an occasion what *can* any trumpery laches on the part of a man or woman matter?" After which magnanimous query the widower left the room, made his way downstairs, secured his hat, and, grasping Mr. Gayre by the hand, departed in the most cheerful spirits, producing a great effect on all the persons he met by his lugubrious countenance and the persistent manner in which he shook his head, as though he had tried a wrestle with grief and been sorely worsted in the struggle.

No man was perhaps ever more astonished than Mr. Sudlow when he read in the *Times* the death of "Margaret, wife of Sir Geoffrey Chelston, Bart., deeply lamented by her sorrowing and affectionate husband." He was so much astounded, indeed, that he found it necessary to call at North Bank where there was no one to receive him except Lavender, from whom he failed, to extract any save the most ordinary answers.

"He had known Lady Chelston—yes, well; he remembered her home-coming and the great doings at the Pleasaunce. She was a beautiful lady—more beautiful, according to Mr. Lavender's ideas, if he might say so without offence, even than Miss Chelston. Her married life, he thought he might go so far as to confess, could not have been a happy one. You know Sir

Geoffrey, sir," Lavender proceeded to remark,
" and it is not all ladies who could make
allowance for his ways." Anyhow, they
didn't agree, and they lived apart. It
was better for married folk to live apart
if they didn't live happily together. The
Baronet was gone down to Chelston to
arrange about the funeral. None but
intimate friends were to be present (and
something in the man's manner informed
Mr. Sudlow he was not going to be asked,
and that Lavender knew it). Miss Chelston
(who at that moment of speaking happened
to be upstairs closeted with her dress-
maker), was out of town. Her grief was
terrible ; though she had not seen her
ladyship for years, still, in Lavender's
opinion, a mother was a mother, and, as
Mr. Sudlow put the question so straight,
he did not think Sir Geoffrey ought to
have kept his daughter all to himself as
he had done. Latterly there had been a

talk of Miss Chelston living for part of the year with her mamma. Lavender had always heard Lady Chelston was a great heiress; most likely her fortune would come to her daughter, but even Lavender's wisdom could not tell exactly how that might be;" and then Mr. Lavender, with a grave face and sad subdued manner, shut the gate after Mr. Sudlow, and went back into the house, and had a laugh with his wife over the suitor's discomfiture.

"I can't abear him," said Mrs. Lavender.

"Nor me," agreed Lavender; "but he's better than nobody, I suppose, and I do hear he's rolling in riches."

Meantime Mr. Gayre had returned to England, and in the large dining-room of his house in Wimpole Street his sister's body lay ready for burial. For several reasons Mr. Moreby's villa seemed ineligible for so rare a purpose, and it scarcely needed Sir Geoffrey's hint that any day the bailiffs might enter into possession, which "would be confoundedly awkward, you know," to decide the banker as to the course he should pursue.

"Sorrowing and affectionate," considered Mr. Gayre, reading the announcement in the *Times.* "I daresay! And now Sir Geoffrey Chelston, Baronet, who so deeply laments his dead wife, is eligible once again, what will he do with this chance, I wonder?"

Sir Geoffrey could have told him that the first thing he meant to do was to offer himself and title to Mrs. Jubbins; but his *rôle* was to keep up the semblance of distracted grief for poor Margaret, and no man understood the beauty and wisdom of silence better than the bereaved husband. So far grief had returned him excellent interest. Mr. Wookes instantly placed, not merely the family vault, but also Chelston Pleasaunce, at his service. Mrs. Wookes, and the young person Sir Geoffrey with a deep sigh styled her "lovely daughter," were introduced to the worthy Baronet. Mr. Wookes spoke of him as "my afflicted friend," and he was earnestly requested to stop and partake of "some refreshment," which, under an immense delusion, he certainly would have done, had he not been compelled to hurry off to catch the afternoon express.

"There are so many things to see to at such a time," he said; and Mrs. Wookes sighed, "Ah, yes, there are!" and Miss Wookes stared at him hard with wide-open colourless eyes; and Mr. Wookes insisted he and Mr. Gayre should come down the evening before the funeral and stay the night; and "whenever you feel disposed to stop with us, I can assure you, Sir Geoffrey, both Mrs. Wookes and myself will give you a hearty welcome," added Mr. Wookes, who, though truly pious, would have welcomed Lucifer himself had he come with a handle to his name.

"I really do not know how to thank you sufficiently," answered Sir Geoffrey, in his best manner, which Mrs. Wookes often subsequently defined as "courtly," though she might have employed a different word had the Baronet been a tutor. "My daughter will be delighted when she hears I met with such a reception at her old home."

"How is Miss Chelston?" instantly inquired Mr. Wookes.

"She is dreadfully cut up, poor thing, of course," explained Sir Geoffrey. "Still, she tries not to let me see all she feels."

Then Mr. Wookes, in a grand pompous voice, immediately said, "My dear;" and Mrs. Wookes understanding observed, "Yes,

I was just about to remark that if dear Miss Chelston thought a change to so quiet a place would do her good, we should feel honoured by a visit;" after which amenities, Sir Geoffrey took a hurried leave, and entered the conveyance waiting for him; first, *sotto voce*, desiring the coachman to " drive to Chelston Station like the——"

There is no time probably which passes so slowly as that intervening between a death and a funeral, but at length the interval was well-nigh bridged over by a succession of weary hours; and the evening arrived when Mr. Wookes was to be gratified with the presence of his " distinguished " guest and that guest's less distinguished brother-in-law.

" I hope they've some decent wine," said Mr. Geoffrey, as the gates swung wide to welcome the visitors. " He looks like an old boy who knows what's what, and the cellars here are first-rate."

"It might have been prudent to bring some cognac with you," suggested Mr. Gayre, with a fine sneer.

"O, I'll square the butler!" answered Sir Geoffrey amiably; and then he looked out of the carriage-window and shook his head, and remarked his heart was well-nigh broken, by —, it was! to think poor Margaret was not to be carried from the house which properly belonged to her. "It may be partly my own fault. I was always too easy and generous, and never thought enough of myself; but, gad, that makes it no pleasanter to see a place like this owned by a fellow who made his money out of tallow, and to have to ask leave to bury my wife in my own vault, cap in hand, like a railway porter;" which recital of misfortunes was ended by their arrival at the house, where Mr. Wookes in person appeared at the door to greet them, and to tell Mr. Gayre how delighted he felt to welcome

any relation of his " esteemed friend Sir
Geoffrey Chelston."

" You'd like a cup of tea, perhaps, before
you go up to dress," he said, with genial
hospitality. " I always find a cup of tea
so refreshing after a railway journey. There
was a time when I would have proposed a
glass of wine ; but we've changed all that
—we are strict abstainers."

" And so not merely virtuous yourselves,
but the cause of virtue in others," observed
Mr. Gayre, scarcely able to repress a smile
at the sight of his brother-in-law's discomfiture. For a moment, indeed, Sir Geoffrey
was too deeply indignant to speak ; but he
regained his presence of mind during the
course of some didactic remarks from Mr.
Wookes concerning the prevalence of drunk-
enness, and the importance of the upper
classes setting an example of temperance to
the masses.

" You are quite right, Mr. Wookes,"

agreed the Baronet, who had already set his wits to work to consider how he could get some brandy " or—or anything, by Jove," from Chelston. " People do drink far too much—and eat to," added Sir Geoffrey as a happy after-thought, feeling he was clear of the vice of gluttony, at any rate.

Mr. Wookes reddened. He liked to see a good table, and to partake plentifully of what he called " God's mercies " spread upon it.

" As for eating," he observed, " though we cannot deny that it is a sin to indulge any appetite to excess, still I consider that a moderate pleasure in and use of the bounties so lavishly provided for our benefit are not crimes. You see, my dear sir," and he laid a fat pudgy hand affectionately on Sir Geoffrey's arm, " the difference is this— fish, flesh, and fowl, vegetables of all sorts, and sweets at discretion, do not cause

quarrelling and murders; whereas spirits—
and under the general head of spirits I in-
clude all sorts of wine—*Won't* you have
a cup of tea?" he broke off to ask, feeling,
perhaps, his arguments might seem a little
lengthy to hungry and thirsty men.

"Thank you; I should like one greatly,"
answered Mr. Gayre.

"And I'd like a glass of *water*," declared
the Baronet desperately, "to lay the dust.
My throat is as dry as a London street in
summer."

"Ah! that's because you are in such
trouble," sympathetically said Mr. Wookes,
who knew as well as possible Sir Geoffrey
was one of the hardest drinkers in England,
and who would have liked to offer him
champagne had his new principles not been
dearer to him even than a title.

They were, indeed, as new as his possession of the Pleasaunce, and he had been
frightened into them by the sudden decease

of a brother, who died, as one City wag
expressed the matter to another, "of forgetting to put any water in his grog."

There is no bigot like a convert (pervert
Sir Geoffrey would have said), and Mr. and
Mrs. Wookes were already anxious to begin
the holy labour of washing this Ethiop
white. They belonged to the straitest sect:
not a pint of beer was allowed about the
premises; dinners were cooked, and horses
driven, and tables set, and fruit forced,
and gardens kept in order on the strictest
teetotal lines. The lodge-keepers drank
nothing stronger than milk ("like babes
and sucklings," said the Baronet afterwards, in accents of the deepest disgust);
no labourers were employed who refused
to give up malt liquor. Indeed, Mr. Wookes
had drawn such a cordon of sobriety round
his domain that when Sir Geoffrey, during
the course of the evening, made an excuse
for stealing out, he found the very beer-

house in the little village hard by had been closed, and the premises converted into a coffee-tavern.

"Well, I'm blanked!" he thought; and, making the best of a bad bargain, decided he would go back and render himself agreeable to "old mother" Wookes, and get something definite settled about Peggy's visit to The Pleasaunce.

This was how he chanced to be " fasting from everything but sin," when he attended his wife's funeral, and shed those tears that excited the surprise and won the admiration of all beholders.

"Tell you what, Gayre," he said, as they returned together to London, " another day in that house would have killed me. It was inhuman too, under the circumstances —downright inhuman, and confoundedly impertinent into the bargain. A man has a right perhaps to play tricks with his own constitution, but he has no right to try to leave another man with no stomach to speak of. *I* shouldn't force a fellow who came to my house to drink against his will. Why should I be compelled to swallow gallons of cold water?—bad as a drench, begad! Why, you see yourself the effect it had upon me. Whatever I might feel— and, as a rule, people haven't thought I felt much—they were mistaken, though—I could control myself; but I give you my word, Gayre, I am still as shaky as possible. I could cry like a woman now. It was an awful ordeal! But the poor dear, could she have seen, would, I think, have understood I bore no malice, and that I loved her to the last—I did, upon my soul!" And the Baronet once again took to weeping so profusely his brother-in-law began anxiously to examine the time-table, to see how soon they might hope to reach a " civilized station," to quote Sir Geoffrey, " where stimulants could be procured."

"I'm a fool," said the widower, wiping his red eyes, "an utter idiot; but the whole thing has been too much for me. I do think all the people behaved splendidly. Fancy, even old Dane coming—though, perhaps, that was as much to prove he didn't care about his grandson being in gaol as to show respect to Margaret's memory."

"He looks a dreadful old man," observed Mr. Gayre, wisely passing over his brother-in-law's final suggestion.

"He looks what he is. Only to think of that poor young fellow having to break stones, or carry stones, or whatever it may be, for seven long years at Portland, and this old wretch gloating over the guineas he can't take out of the world with him, and that might have saved the lad! Why such things should be allowed baffles me! And that dear poor Susan coming down here to ask him to help get up a petition, or a memorial, or something of the sort, and the wretch as good as shutting the door in her face! Drummond told me about it at the station just now. Give you my word, I scarcely knew how to contain myself."

"What can you mean?" asked Mr. Gayre; "What is Miss Drummond doing?"

"As I understand, the solicitor who acted for young Dane told her if she got a whole lot of influential people to sign a paper, and forwarded it to one or other of the big wigs, she might get the sentence commuted. I don't believe a word of it myself; but still the notion may serve to comfort her a bit till the worst of the trouble had worn off. One thing, however, I am sure of—the girl oughtn't to be going about herself asking for signatures. I wish I had time and money to take such a labour off her hands;" and the Baronet looked hard at Mr. Gayre, who, after a few moments' silence, said,

"I think I am the person to help Miss Drummond now."

"You're the best fellow living, Gayre!" exclaimed Sir Geoffrey, giving his brother-in-law such a slap on the shoulder that the banker winced. "I always said it and I always thought it, spite of some few angularities—and which of us is perfect?—you are the kindest, and the most generous, and the truest man in England." Having finished which peroration, as the train stopped, the Baronet jumped out of the compartment at the civilised station, and returned refreshed.

CHAPTER XI.

A DOG IN THE MANGER.

INSTEAD of formally offering the "assistance of his experience" by letter, Mr. Gayre decided to call upon Miss Drummond, and actually got within twenty yards of the house at Shepherd's Bush, when he suddenly hesitated, turned and commenced retracing his steps.

"What can it be?" he thought. "From the moment I first saw this girl a power stronger than myself seemed drawing me towards her; and yet at the very same moment some spirit of prescience said, "if you allow your inclinations to lead you now, you will in the future repent having done so." It is odd, very odd, at each turn of the affair a check or warning has met me; and now, here again, almost with my foot on the doorstep, I feel I cannot meet her this morning—feel almost as though I could wish we had never met. Her influence upon me too is not for good; strange, because she is all good! If there be any lasting virtue to be extracted out of my scheming brother-in-law (which I doubt), she could extract it. Though Sudlow hates her, he thinks it necessary to be on his best behaviour when she is present. The fair Peggy also is an atom more human, less affected, less straitlaced, altogether less unendurable when Susan makes one of the party. But, so far as I am concerned, it is really only since I knew her I feel capable of treason, stratagem or spoil. If I could be sure of not being found out I would rob my neighbour, cheat my friend, commit a murder, and see an innocent man hanged for my deed, supposing any one of those acts would bring me closer to Susan. Then, when I married her, I should, I have no doubt, find she had all unconsciously brought the avenging sword to church with her. I wonder whether all this is temptation? I am half inclined to think so! For generations we have been such a lot of respectable Pharisees that no doubt it needed an angel to teach us we are only common clay, subject to like temptations, &c. But hold! What about poor Margaret? Is Sir Geoffrey an angel—was Sir Geoffrey ever an angel? Here is a difficult conundrum—Why do I feel myself a worse man since I have known Susan Drummond? Is it because she is a good woman? Pooh! what will the end of all this be, I wonder? Will time solve the riddle? I have a strong belief in the ability of time to solve most riddles, and— Ah, d'ye do,

Sudlow? who would have expected to meet you here?"

"I am often in this neighbourhood; but you—"

"Set out to call on Miss Drummond, and then changed my mind."

"Indeed! You would not have found her at home, however, if you had called."

"O!"

"She is staying at the Wigwam."

"Is my niece there too?"

Mr. Sudlow shook his head.

"Sir Geoffrey means to lunch with Mrs. Jubbins to-day."

"Does he know Miss Drummond is at Chislehurst?"

"Of course; it was he told me."

Having successfully planted which thorn in the banker's bosom, Mr. Sudlow proceeded on his way, pleased to have scored even so poor a trick.

"He's jealous of his own shadow," con-

sidered the careful young man. "If it
wasn't that my lady would snub me so
dreadfully, I'd have a turn at making love
to her myself, in order to vex the Baronet
and drive Gayre mad. Marry him! The
money is not in Lombard Street would
buy her *yet:* and when the time comes
that it might, our dear friend will have
found out practically roses wither and
lilies fade."

"Sir Geoffrey will tell her she may depend on my help, and so spoil the whole
effect," thought Mr. Gayre, with a feeling of savage disappointment. "Well,
things must take their chance now. I can
only wait results."

He had not long to wait. It was about
a quarter to four on the same afternoon—
the busiest part of a banker's day, only
Mr. Gayre was not busy—when a clerk
took a card into that gentleman's private
office, intimating at the same time the lady

whose name it bore " would like to speak
to him."

Mr. Gayre's first impulse was to rise
and rush out to greet this unexpected
visitor; but prudence prevailed, and in
his coldest business tone he desired that
Miss Drummond might be asked to walk
in.

Then he waited—waited till he heard
the rustle of Susan's dress, as she drew
nearer and nearer; waited till the door
opened, and he heard the clerk's warning
to beware of that step, which so often
caused a customer or possible client to
enter the sacred apartment with an un-
dignified stumble. Then he rose; he
could refrain no longer.

" Pray be careful, Miss Drummond," he
said; " that step is so very awkward. I
must really have it altered." And then
it flashed through his mind, if Susan
would only promise to marry him, he

might, even at so late a period of his life, alter many things, beginning with himself, for example.

That was, indeed, a moment to be marked with a white stone in the banker's memory. The woman he loved stood there looking with her soft brown eyes, from which the remembered sunshine had departed, up into his face, with a sort of timid appeal that wrung a heart not over susceptible to the troubles of others. She had come to him voluntarily for help. It was the beginning of the end. It was for this he had turned back almost from the threshold of her home. That which he so foolishly construed into a warning proved to be an omen for good—an omen already fulfilled.

"I fear," she began—and there was a hesitation in her manner he had never previously seen in it—"I fear I am intruding, Mr. Gayre. I walked twice up and down Lombard Street before I could summon sufficient courage to ask for you."

He did not answer this remark for a moment. The contrast between the girl, strong in her fearless innocence, he had sauntered with on that memorable night beneath the stars at Chislehurst and this stricken Susan, who had since faced the then intangible evil she vaguely felt was advancing to meet her, seemed to him so cruel he could not find words in which to clothe his pity.

When he did speak it was lightly.

"Strange to say, I went almost to Miss Matthews' door this morning, intending to call upon you; but then I turned back, fearing to intrude—"

"I am not with Miss Matthews now."

"No, so I understand; but I was unaware you had gone to Chislehurst till I heard from Mr. Sudlow you were staying at the Wigwam."

"I shall only be there till to-morrow. I have taken lodgings at Islington."

"At Islington! Why? Forgive me; of course I have no right to ask."

"Certainly you have every right. You want to know why I left Miss Matthews. We disagreed—about Oliver. I could not bear it—I could not. Everybody is sorry for me; but nobody is sorry for him. Now I don't want people to be sorry for me."

"No one could help being sorry for you," said the banker, gently.

She looked at him for an instant questioningly; then tears welled up into her eyes, and she turned her head aside as she said,

"I have come to ask you to help me, Mr. Gayre. It is very bold of me, perhaps, but—"

"I went to Shepherd's Bush this morning to know if you would not let me try to help you."

"How could you know I wanted help?"

" Sir Geoffrey told me. He said you
were endeavouring to get some petition
signed. That is so, is it not ? "

"Yes. And O, Mr. Gayre, if you will
only put me in the way of getting the right
people to sign it, I shall be unutterably
grateful."

"Anything I can do for you, be sure I
will do."

"Thank you !—I feel certain of that.
And you won't advise me ; I am so tired of
being advised—so weary of hearing I ought
to sit down and fold my hands and do
nothing, while he—is—and we were all the
world to one another ! "

"I shall not advise you," said Mr. Gayre,
who felt no inclination to mingle his tears
with the girl over the woes of Oliver Dane.
" Only tell me what you are doing--what
you want done--and I will assist you to the
best of my ability."

" How kind you are ! " she cried—" how

good! I will try to explain how it all came about. But I fear I am taking up your time. You are busy, are you not? I had better write to you—may I?

"Might I not call upon you, Miss Drummond? I shall be most happy to do so, if you name an hour convenient to yourself."

"*Any* hour," answered Susan—"any hour which suits you. I do feel grateful, though I cannot express my gratitude. How can I ever be thankful enough to God for raising up such a friend for me in my extremity?" Which, being a question Mr. Gayre, under the most favourable circumstances, could scarcely have been expected to answer, he prudently affected not to hear.

"I may be fortunate enough to see you at Chislehurst this evening," he said, instead of solving that difficult problem as to whether Miss Drummond, if she could read his heart, might regard his friendship in the light of an unmixed blessing. "I was thinking of calling at The Wigwam. Then, perhaps you will kindly give me your address, and let me know when I should be most certain to find you at home."

" But please do not mention the matter before Mrs. Jubbins," entreated Susan. " She does not say anything, but I know she is like every one else."

" Surely not *every one!* There are exceptions."

" Yes, I forgot. Sir Geoffrey, of course— kind good Sir Geoffrey."

"Won't you bracket us together, Miss Drummond ? "

She looked at him searchingly for a moment before she asked,

" Do you believe Oliver to be innocent, then ? "

The question was put with such direct suddenness that Mr. Gayre found it difficult to parry.

"It is not easy to believe him innocent,"
he answered; "but—pray do not mis-
understand me, Miss Drummond—I do not
say he is guilty. Appearances are often
against a man; and this is a case in which I,
for one, should not care to express a positive
opinion. Of one thing, however, I am
certain—that, whether the verdict were
righteous or unrighteous, the sentence was
utterly beyond the offence; and, without
going into the question of guilt or innocence,
I will do all I can to help you and him.
You must not be angry with me," added the
banker apologetically, "because I have not
the same faith in Mr. Dane you possess.
Remember, I never was intimate with him
in the slightest degree—"

"That is true," she murmured; "had you
known you could not have doubted him."

"Besides," said Mr. Gayre, finishing his
interrupted sentence, "I have seen something of the world, and understand how

temptation assails, and often overcomes, even the very best amongst us."

" It did not overcome him," declared Susan.

" Then on your word I am to believe Mr. Dane sinned against, not sinning : is that so ? "

" If you can."

" I will do precisely what you tell me. I consider myself a soldier under orders, and shall hold no personal opinions whatever. I think I had better let you out by this private door. You would of course rather avoid passing through the bank. Good-bye for the present, Miss Drummond —no, please, don't thank me. If we meet at The Wigwam perhaps it might be more prudent to say nothing about your having been here. Once more, good-bye; depend I will do all in my power for your friend."

And in another second Susan was once again in Lombard Street, with the old dull pain tugging at her heart, spite of the faith she had in Mr. Gayre's power to help young Dane, and the certainty she felt he would try to do so.

"But O, he cannot be of the use he might if he only believed in my darling!" she considered.

When, some two hours later, Mr. Gayre arrived at Chislehurst it was scarcely agreeable to find Sir Geoffrey acting as Mentor to the youth of the family, who were listening to his improving stories with enthusiasm, and encoring reminiscences of flood and field in a manner which should have been gratifying to the Baronet.

"She can't bear these old tales now," said Sir Geoffrey, *sotto voce*, to his brother-in-law, indicating Susan, who was seated apart in the larger drawing-room; "but she'll mend of that, poor soul. It has been worse than a death to her. You must give her time, Gayre—give her time."

42—2

"Good Heavens! have I ever interfered with her in any way?" asked the banker.

"No, no; I didn't mean that. Only *verbum sap.*, a nod's as good as a wink, you know, and I really do love Susan like my own child."

"And what was done to the mare that broke her leg, when old Carey would take him over the bullfinch, Sir Geoffrey?" inquired one of the younger Jubbins.

"Shot, Joshua—dead as a doornail. A rough sort of fellow, Poaching Bill he was called, happened to come up at the minute, and we sent him for a pistol to put the poor brute out of his misery. Give you my word there was not a dry eye in the field, except old Carey's. 'I said I'd teach her who was master,' declared the gray-haired ruffian, 'and I did it.'"

"If you had broken your own neck it wouldn't have mattered," I remarked; "but by—, sir, you've killed the finest mare in the county, and if the other gentlemen present are of my mind, you may hunt the county by yourself for the future. Fair riding is one thing, and fair punishment is one thing; but brutality's another, and Geoffrey Chelston will never eat bread nor shake hands with a man who has done a gallant animal to death, as you've tortured one this day."

"And did he hunt the county by himself?" asked the pertinacious Joshua.

"No, my lad; he went to another county, where they would have none of him either. The story followed him—I took precious good care it should—and so, at last, the talk and disgrace broke his own heart. His dying words, I understand, were, "Curse Chelston!" but I didn't care for that. I always say, if you do right, no man's bad opinion need trouble you. And now, you see, Carey's in his grave, and I'm telling the story of his wicked cruelty to a set of boys who ought to know how to go across country as well as I do. If you'll persuade your mother to let you come down and see me at Chelston— But there, what am I talking about? Well, well, though I haven't The Pleasaunce any longer, you ought to know how to take your fences. There's Gayre, now; d'ye suppose he's a bit worse banker because he's as straight a rider as you'd wish to see? Gad, Nicholas, shall I ever forget seeing that wild Irish devil— that chestnut mare, Leda, I mean—take you first over the ha-ha, with only one foot in your stirrups, and then across the Chel, before you were fairly settled in your saddle? By Jove, it was as fine a bit of horsemanship as ever came in my way! She took the notion in her head and went for it; and there was Margaret screaming, and the grooms running, and I expecting you'd be brought back dead; and then you just turned the creature's pretty head—Lord, what a thing memory is! I seem to have that star on her forehead before my eyes this minute—and brought her back the way she had gone, gentle as a lamb."

With which, and suchlike pleasing and instructive anecdotes, the Baronet held the youthful Jubbins entranced during the compulsory absence of their mamma, who, in honour of Sir Geoffrey's presence, had proceeded to her room, in order to don a more elaborate dinner-dress.

The feeling Mrs. Jubbins entertained towards the brothers-in-law was, to a certain extent, contradictory. Whilst Mr. Gayre remained the love of her heart, she felt a pride concerning the easy and familiar terms on which Sir Geoffrey honoured The Wigwam with his presence she did not even try to disguise. The names of great persons grew to be as common on her lips as in the columns of the *Court Journal.* She repeated anecdotes of the nobility to her friends on the authority of the Baronet, which were not really more untruthful than such anecdotes usually are. The private history and daily life of no peer of the realm remained a sealed book to her. Thanks to good Sir Geoffrey, she was *au fait* with everything which occurred at Windsor and Balmoral. she felt that a visit even from the Prince of Wales would not quite have overwhelmed her. She had heard how his Royal Highness was in the habit of greeting her friend at Ascot with " Geoffrey, my boy," and " Chelston, old fellow," and asking his advice concerning which horse the Princess should back for a dozen of gloves. As for the younger Jubbins, they were simply rapturous on the subject of Sir Geoffrey.

In his charming way he had pinched the girls' cheeks, and declared they were " deyv'lish good-looking," " pretty little things," " that when they went to Court they would put some persons noses out, begad!" with a

good deal more to the same edifying
effect.

He got a pony on which Miss Ida could
canter as easily as if she was sitting in an
armchair in her mother's drawing-room, and
himself accompanied that young lady while
she ambled along the Kentish lanes. He
sent Lavender frequently to The Wigwam,
so that the smaller fry might under his
auspices learn to fall easy on the velvet
turf once pressed by the august feet of Lady
Merioneth. He told the lads stories of his
own exploits and the exploits of other
worthies like himself, and promised that
when he " pulled his affairs together a bit "
he " would make men of them." He proposed furnishing a sort of armoury at Lord
Flint's former abode, which excellent idea had,
however, to be abandoned in consequence
of Mrs. Jubbins' nervous terror of firearms.

" Why, my dear soul," he said to that lady,
" if you'd only let me take you in hand, I'd

engage you should in a month hit at a hundred yards."

"I never said what she'd hit," he confided to his brother-in-law; "but it did not matter because she thinks everything with a muzzle can bite, and is deadly afraid even of a toy pistol. Those big women always are cowards —ever notice that? Courage decreases as fat is laid on—fact, I assure you."

In a sentence, then, the Baronet had secured the favour of the whole establishment. With the men and women servants his rank and agreeable manners made him, as a matter of course, prime favourite. No standing aloof with him.

"About people of real good birth there is never no nasty low sort of pride," declared the united voice of the servants' hall.

Even the cattle within Mrs. Jubbins' gates evinced a discriminating partiality for so worthy a gentleman.

"They're like children, bless you," he said,

to Mrs. Jubbins, in kindly explanation. " They know who is fond of them. Why, look at your young folks! (Gad! who'd think you were old enough to be their mother?) They'll leave any of your rich friends, your City magnates rolling in money, to come and stroll about with me, poor as I am. They respect Nicholas Gayre, Banker, but they like Geoffrey Chelston, Beggar— that's about it."

Concerning his wife, Geoffrey Chelston, Beggar, had fairly mystified Mrs. Jubbins. In broken accents he had formerly told how a reconciliation was imminent ; how he had been a very bad boy, who meant now to turn over a new leaf—upon his soul he did ; how Gayre was the best fellow living ; how Margaret could be regarded but as little lower than the angels ; what a wretch he had been to the best woman who ever lived ; with a great deal more to the same effect, which often caused the widow to wonder if that

great trouble which bowed old Mr. Gayre's
gray head, and left Sir Geoffrey's little
daughter motherless, had been all a dream.

In their first shame and misery the Gayres
were unable to hide the sorrow which had
fallen on them within their own breasts; but
now, to hear Sir Geoffrey, any one might
have thought all the sin and scandal were of
his own making.

"He is certainly most magnanimous," said
the widow, to Mr. Gayre.

"*Most* magnanimous!" agreed the banker,
with an irony perfectly unintelligible to Mrs.
Jubbins. "He is quite willing to let bygones
be bygones; so is Margaret, and so am
I."

"I think it may prove a comfort to the
poor girl to have some old friend to whom
she can speak," explained the Baronet, to his
brother-in-law. "The Jubbins is not much,
to be sure; but she means well and is
faithful, and will serve better at first than

nobody. 'Pon my honour, Gayre, I like the widow; for her rank, indeed for any rank, she is a most excellent sort of person."

She was indeed so excellent a sort of person, Sir Geoffrey thought, after his wife's death, he could not do better than confide a few of the many troubles besetting him to her. "And now the poor dear's gone and all that's knocked on the head, and the link which bound Gayre to us is broken, what is to become of Peggy God only knows. As for me it does not matter; I can make shift anywhere. Great happiness has never come to me, and I needn't expect happiness now. I did look forward to some peace and quietness with Margaret; but she has gone to that bourne—you have read *Hamlet*, of course, Mrs. Jubbins?"

Mrs. Jubbins said she had seen it acted, and that she felt very sorry for Ophelia. Upon the whole, the Baronet gathered, she considered Hamlet rather a foolish young man, and his mamma a most dreadful and wicked person.

"Only think of the unprincipled creature marrying again in that way!" she remarked.

"Only think of people marrying again in any way!" capped the Baronet; "I couldn't, I know. That is a point I have always admired especially about you, Mrs. Jubbins. It is not often one meets a woman young, rich, handsome, calculated to adorn society, resolute as you are to wear the willow, even for the best husband that ever lived."

"Ah, but where would you find so good a husband as mine was?" sighed the widow.

"Nowhere—nowhere," promptly agreed Sir Geoffrey. "I have heard things from Gayre about your husband that make me lament I did not know him." And then the Baronet, after accepting an invitation to stop for dinner, walked off to find some of his young friends; while Mrs. Jubbins hastened away to change her dress, considering, as she did so, that poor dear Mr. J. always did like her to "look her best."

But for Sir Geoffrey, the dinner would have passed off very heavily. He, however, proved the life of the party.

"A most agreeable gentleman," said Hoskins, as he descended to the basement, "as I am sure I shall always be the first to admit. Nevertheless——"

"Nevertheless what?" demanded Mrs. Jubbins' own maid.

"Things aren't what they was," observed Mr. Hoskins, oracularly. "The position is changed, if I may so express myself. The events of the last fortnight has altered the relations of parties. We can't stand still, Miss Lambton."

"That's true enough," agreed the cook. "If wages ain't rising they're falling, which I will maintain to my dying day."

" Well, and if we can't stand still, what
then ? " asked Miss Lambton.

Mr. Hoskins closed one eye with decorous
solemnity ere answering.

" Least said soonest mended. Though I
have a high opinion of a gentleman who
shall be nameless, his manners being agreeable, his taste in wine as good as my own,
and himself open-handed, I do not altogether
know that it is a match to which I could
give an unqualified approval. There is
wheels within wheels, Miss Lambton ; and I
have heard a word or two drop which might
render caution necessary."

" Get along with you, do ! " expostulated
the cook. " Missus ain't going to make a
fool of herself, though other people may
choose to make fools of themselves ; " which
was a very unkind allusion to the fact that
Mr. Hoskins meant, ere long, to take Miss
Lambton and a public-house, both for better
or w e, and leave " a good place, where he

had nobody to trouble him, for a wife who did not know how to cook a potato and a landlord certain to call for his rent regular."

At that very instant the genial Baronet, who during the whole of dinner-time had been on his very best behaviour, was saying to Mrs. Jubbins' sons,

"Look here, my lads! I promised your mother I would not let you sit long over dessert; and, as I don't want to lose any of your agreeable company, why, we'll all make a move. One minute, Gayre," he added, as his brother-in-law, acting on the hint, rose all too willingly; "I have a word for your private ear. Let the young fellows go. We'll be after you immediately."

And then the dining-room door closed; and, literally in the twinkling of an eye, Sir Geoffrey had poured out and swallowed a bumper of sound Madeira.

"It's a sin to put a wine like that c   .e

table when there's no one to drink it but
women and boys, who would just as soon
have a sweet sherry. But that's not what
I kept you back for—it's not, upon my
conscience. I wanted to tell you I saw
Susan slip into your Bank to-day. Nay,
never fire up, man; surely sight is as free as
the street; and, indeed, I was glad to see the
poor little soul had turned to you in her
trouble. I meant to tell her she'd nothing
to do in this case but ask and have; but the
chance did not offer. So, as I was saying, I
saw her pop up your steps just like a hunted
hare. But Mum's the word as regards me;
and, were I in your place, Mum should be
the word too."

"I have not a notion what you are driving at, "exclaimed Mr. Gayre, testily. "Why
can't you say what you have got to say
in plain English, and be done with it?"

"O! hang me, that's too good!" laughed
the Baronet, at the same time, as if in

very excess of mirth, jocundly seizing the
Madeira decanter, and filling out another
bumper. "Do you know, Gayre," he went
on, "I have heard some fool advance the
opinion that the more a man drinks the
less he understands about wine. Did you
ever hear such rubbish? Why, the more
a man drinks, of course, the better judge
he becomes. Practice makes perfect. I
don't suppose even you grasped the whole
science and mystery of money-changing at
the first intention."

"That is a matter into which I really
must decline to enter at present. Mrs.
Jubbins will be wondering what is detain-
ing us."

"I'll explain that I had to speak to you
on a matter of business — and so I have.
Don't you talk about Susan or Susan's
affairs to the widow. She's an excellent
person, no doubt—I'm sure I have no cause
to say one word against her; but in all

these City folks there's a deuced hard ker-
nel; and she wouldn't approve, and she'd
launch out on **poor** dear Susan, and she'd
advise and preach and talk against Dane;
and then they'd **quarrel,** and Susan would
close another door between herself and her
friends. She's just **in the** humour to fight
anybody **for the** sake of Dane; and, Lord,
what use is it? By the way, why *don't*
you marry her?"

"What do you mean? Marry whom?"

"The widow, to be sure."

"You might as well ask me why I don't
fly to the moon; the one inquiry is about
as reasonable **as the** other."

"Don't think so. In the first place, you
don't want to fly to the moon; in the next,
you couldn't fly there if you wished ever so
much. Now, you could marry the widow,
and you have led her to believe you meant
to do so."

"I utterly deny it."

" That is all very well; but she expects you to ask her, and so do her friends. As far as I am a judge, they are only waiting for the word."

" Surely I am not answerable for their expectations."

" Yes, you are—to a great extent at any rate. Unless a man means business he has no right to fool around a house in which there is an eligible woman, as you have been circling about The Warren. Gad! if I'd been her brother, I'd have had something definite out of you long ago. And when all that is settled, why the deuce shouldn't you marry her? She is as well born as you—both of you are the children of respectable citizens. If her father did go wrong, your father might have gone wrong. Heavens! which of us has a right to throw stones? I don't know how rich you may be, but she is rich enough in all conscience even for a lord to marry ; and if you took

a house in some neighbourhood away from
that vile City connection, and gradually got
rid of the young fry—perhaps put one of
the sons in the bank—and made a quite
fresh start in the country, I feel confident
you might get amongst the best county
people.   It's never too late to mend ! and
if I were you I'd try to have some value
for my money even at the eleventh hour
—I would, upon my soul !   The widow is
certainly both personable and presentable.
I've seen worse driving to a Drawing-room.
Besides—"

"It is really exceedingly kind of you to
take such an unselfish interest in my affairs,
but—" Mr. Gayre tried to interrupt.

"Unselfish !   Not a bit of it, as you'll
know when you let me finish what I was
going to say.   There's Peggy, now.   If you
married the widow, see what a home there
would be for her—that is if you liked to
ask her to the house."

" She and Mrs. Jubbins don't exactly hit matters off," observed Mr. Gayre, maliciously.

" That's true at the present moment ; but if Mrs. Jubbins were Mrs. Gayre, you'd see she'd take even to Peg to please Peg's uncle. 'Pon my soul, Gayre, the woman worships you—that's the plain state of the case ; and why, for very gratitude's sake, you don't make her your wife passes my comprehension. It's not as if there were anybody else."

" No, it is not as though there were anybody else," agreed Mr. Gayre, in a spirit of the bitterest sarcasm.

" And then think of all the good you may do. Why, to go no further, you'd be able to offer poor Susan a rest for the sole of her foot—"

" Better at once start an Asylum for the Fatherless and Afflicted," suggested the banker.

" You might do worse," said Sir Geoffrey,

who had by this time emptied the decanter. "What greater happiness can a man desire than the welfare of his fellow-creatures? That is a point you rich fellows are somewhat apt to overlook; and yet what is the use of money unless you can do some good with it? For my own part, if I were well off—which, of course, I never expect to be now—I'd at once begin to consider how I could best spend part of my wealth as a sort of thank-offering — you understand."

"If you have quite finished your remarks, as you have the Madeira," said Mr. Gayre, "I should wish to make one observation."

"One, my dear fellow! A dozen, if you like; I am in no hurry."

"But I am," retorted Sir Geoffrey's "dear fellow." "What I wish to say is this: I have not, and I never had, the smallest intention of marrying Mrs. Jubbins."

"Honour bright?"

" And what is more," persisted Mr. Gayre, ignoring the implied form of asseveration, " I don't mean you to marry her either."

" I wonder what you take me for ! " cried the Baronet, in indignant expostulation— " with my heart still bleeding for the loss of my poor darling! Ah, Gayre, how can you say such things ? Why, the flowers on Margaret's coffin must still be fresh."

" If that is a question pressing upon your mind, you may be very sure they are as dead as she is," answered Mr. Gayre ; " and for the rest, remember what I say — you shall *not* marry Mrs. Jubbins."

" Well, if ever there was a dog in the manger ! " muttered Sir Geoffrey, as he followed his brother-in-law along the corridor.